LAYOVER

OPEN SKIES, BOOK ONE

BECCA JAMESON

ACKNOWLEDGMENTS

Many thanks to my childhood friend Jason, whose name I used in this book. He provided me with amazing details of his time in Desert Storm, including how he acquired his nickname. I used several of these details when writing Layover, and I'm grateful for his contributions.

PROLOGUE

"That one," Libby whispered as she set her elbows on the high-top table where the two women stood and leaned in closer to Christa, her breath hitching.

Christa glanced at Libby and then followed her line of sight. "The tall one?"

"They're all tall. You think it's a requirement or something?" she joked, sitting up straighter. "Maybe there's a height requirement for men who enter the military."

Christa rolled her pale blue eyes and tucked a lock of blond hair behind her ear. "There is no height requirement for the military."

Libby shot her a goofy glance. "I was kidding."

"You're not wrong though. It seems like all of Trent's friends are tall. And built. And…do these guys ever eat junk food?"

The man Libby had her sights on glanced their direction. When he turned his body, she licked her lips. He had on khaki dress pants, a pale-blue, button-down shirt, and loafers. Casual but stylish. Like the rest of the wedding party at Destiny and Trent's rehearsal dinner.

Libby smiled at him. And then she melted a bit when he returned the smile.

Christa jerked her gaze downward and muttered, "Shit. He caught us ogling."

"Ogling? We're downright staring, and I don't care if he did catch us. Me in particular. I hope he's single."

Christa lifted her gaze back to face Libby. Her cheeks were pink, which happened often considering how pale Christa's skin was and how easily she embarrassed. "Does it even matter? If all you care about is a one-night stand with one of these guys, what difference does it make if he's single or not?"

Libby gasped in mock horror. "I'm not stealing some other woman's man." Destiny, one of her best friends and the star of this weekend, hadn't mentioned any of her fiancé Trent's friends being married or even in serious relationships. So Libby wasn't too worried. She was on a mission. Her goal for the night was to choose a willing, handsome, buff guy and then flirt mercilessly with him.

Tomorrow night was when she intended to strike, after the wedding itself. Tonight would be too obvious in this more intimate gathering in the reserved room at the back of an Italian restaurant. Besides, it would be awkward tomorrow if she slept with one of the groomsmen and then had to face him at the wedding.

She was pretty sure the man she'd singled out who was now glancing at her yet again was named Jason Nixon. It was nearly impossible to keep up with any one of Trent's friends' names since half the time he called them by their last name, and the other half of the time he referred to them by their team nickname. But she'd heard them refer to this tall, broad, breath of fresh air as Hatch.

"I don't know how you can possibly set your mind to having sex with a stranger before you've even met him,"

Christa continued, her voice low, her eyes darting around as if the mention of the word sex might cause eyebrows to rise.

"Girl, do you have any idea what kind of men I've dated? I'm twenty-eight years old. My mother has set me up with half the Guatemalan men anywhere close to my age in a thirty-mile radius. Every one of them has been a failure."

Christa giggled. "Your mom *is* persistent."

"That's an understatement. She doesn't seem to grasp that since I was born and raised in Dallas, I spent my life exposed to a far more diverse culture than she's from." Libby glanced at Christa. "The guys she sets me up with are always cocky and macho. They may act perfectly polite when they're around my parents, but as soon as we're alone it's like they puff out their chests and start some sort of mating dance." Libby shuddered at the reminder.

Christa laughed harder. "Don't forget, I've been with you on a few double dates. I've seen this mating dance in action. Your description is hilarious but spot-on."

Libby sighed as she glanced again at Jason. "I want to know what it feels like to be with a man who's more interested in me than himself. That guy..." She nodded once again toward the man who'd grabbed her attention, "...makes me squirm. I like the way he smiles at me. It doesn't hurt that he's rock hard, muscular, and tall." Libby sighed dramatically.

"Not gonna lie. He looks pretty cocky himself."

Libby shook her head. "No. It's different. He looks confident. Alpha, but not in a macho sort of way," she mused. "I've always had a bit of a thing for men in uniform. I'm dying to roll around between the sheets with one of them."

"And you think if you sleep with one of these guys, you'll get it out of your system? Seems like a risky idea."

Libby nodded. "That's my plan."

"What are you going to tell your mom when you end up falling for him?"

Libby cringed. "Not gonna happen. My parents would have a coronary if I dated a man like that cool drink of water. He has so many strikes against him, my mother would drop dead. He's full-blooded American for one thing, and white."

"Might I remind you that you're full-blooded American too," Christa pointed out. "It's not a race."

Libby laughed. "To my mother it is. 'Guatemalans must stick together,'" she began in her mother's authoritative tone. "'It's time for you to find a nice man from our country and settle down. I'm not getting any younger. I need grandbabies.'"

Christa winced. "Yeah, your mom does kinda sound like that."

"And the crazy thing is that she was born in the US too. I guess the fact that she lived in a less diverse community growing up caused her to absorb more of the traditional Guatemalan ways of thinking. I thought maybe she would lighten up after her parents passed away, but noooo. If anything, she lays it on even thicker."

"Shit. He's coming this way," Christa whispered.

Libby sat up straighter, smoothing her hands down her dress, over her thighs. She hoped her makeup looked okay. She hadn't reapplied lipstick since they'd finished dinner.

Suddenly, she felt a bit silly and presumptuous. It wasn't like her to pick out a man from across a room and set her sights on him. She honestly hadn't dated any white guys. Nor had she dated anyone as formidable as this man.

His gaze was definitely set on her as he approached, his swagger slightly cocky, his lips tipped up almost in a smirk. Maybe he was no different than the macho guys she was used to, but somehow he had a different vibe. Her body had come alive more and more throughout the evening. By now, she was buzzing with arousal. Most of the men she'd dated made her cringe and shrink away from them within minutes. Not this one. By the time he reached their table, Libby was no longer breathing. She had to tip her head way back to meet his gaze.

He turned toward Christa. "I haven't had a chance to meet you two yet." He held out a hand. "Jason Nixon."

At least Libby had his name right in her head.

Christa shook his hand in her small pale one, barely managing to murmur, "Christa Boyce." She took a step back, pointing over her shoulder. "I'm just gonna go get a drink." She fled so fast it was a wonder a breeze didn't hit Libby in the face.

Jason turned his attention toward Libby once again and took her hand next. "And you are?"

"Libby. Libby Garcia," she stammered, loving the feel of his firm handshake. His hand was darn near twice the size of hers. Granted, everything about her was petite. She was four eleven and proportionately dainty. Most of the time that fact drove her crazy, and she worked hard to make up for her size with personality. With Jason, she suddenly didn't mind. He seemed huge and powerful, and she liked it.

"Libby. Is that short for Elizabeth?"

She shook her head and cleared her throat. "No. Libertad."

"Ah, Hispanic. Libertad. Liberty. I love that." His accent was nearly perfect.

Her eyes widened. For one thing, no one ever loved her weird name. And for another thing, Jason Nixon apparently spoke at least enough Spanish to correctly pronounce and translate Liberty. *Interesting.* "Thank you," she managed to murmur as he released her fingers.

"Nice to meet you, Libby. Save a dance for me tomorrow night?"

She nearly choked as she stared at his raised eyebrow. She was not going to chicken out. She was so totally going to lay it on thick with this hunk. "Absolutely. Looking forward to it."

CHAPTER 1

Twenty-four hours later...

Libby slid her palms up and down Jason's back as soon as he'd tugged off his uniform jacket and draped it over the back of the one chair in his hotel room. He was as hard as she'd imagined. Every inch of him rock solid. Muscular. Fit. Her mouth watered. A frantic yearning to have more of him consumed her.

He hadn't even kissed her yet, but she could tell by the hungry look in his eyes that was about to change. He cupped her face and stared into her eyes in the dim light.

After hours of flirting mercilessly with each other at the wedding and then the reception, they had finally broken away from the party to sneak upstairs to his room. The sneaking part probably wasn't necessary, nor did she suspect they had pulled it off. She doubted any of her friends or his had any doubt about where and how she and Jason intended to spend the rest of the night.

He stepped closer, taking her breath away as he flattened

her to the wall. His huge hands came to her face, cupping it reverently, his gaze intense. "I'm going to kiss every inch of your body," he informed her in a gravelly voice.

"I hope so," she whispered in response. She'd been aroused all evening. No. She'd been aroused since she'd set eyes on him last night at the rehearsal. She'd tossed and turned all night dreaming about what it might be like to have his hands on her, his lips on hers, his cock inside her.

Thank God he'd gotten the message from her not-so-subtle suggestions last night because she wasn't sure what she might have done if she'd arrived at the wedding today to find him ignoring her entirely.

He'd done nothing of the sort. In fact, when she'd first spotted him among the crowd of groomsmen gathered outside the church, he'd smiled at her. Confident. Knowing.

Her heart had fluttered from that moment on. Thousands of glances later, with no words spoken between them, he'd finally taken her hand and led her to the dance floor near the end of the evening. "You promised me a dance," he'd murmured as he began to rock her back and forth to the slow song.

His hands had been everywhere, sliding up and down her back, over her ass, around to stroke the sides of her breasts. Anyone paying attention would think they were an item. It had been raw. Heady. Exciting.

After three dances in which they'd exchanged only a handful of words, he'd lifted a brow. "Take five minutes to say goodbye to your friends."

Her panties had melted at those words. Not a question. Not even an inquiry. Just a firm demand. She'd shuddered and then licked her lips. "I don't need to. I'll see them tomorrow."

He'd smiled slowly before spinning her around and angling her toward the ballroom exit. "Purse?"

"Nope." She'd left everything in her room upstairs. The

one she was sharing with Christa. Their other two friends, Bex and Shayla, were in the adjoining room. The four of them, along with Destiny, worked for the same airline, Open Skies. That's how they'd met several years ago.

All of Libby's friends were fully aware of her intentions for the night. She'd waxed on and on about wanting to have sex with a military man for years. This was her chance. She was taking it.

She had no doubt the three of them would spend plenty of time teasing her both behind her back tonight and in the morning. She didn't care. This was going to be one of the best nights of her life.

Jason drew her thoughts back to the present when he stroked his thumb over her bottom lip. "Open for me, Libby."

She shivered as she parted her lips, letting his thumb slide inside. Every syllable coming from his mouth made her hotter. Her damn traitorous nipples had been hard all evening under the silky material of her black evening gown. She wasn't wearing a bra, and that heightened her awareness.

None of them had worn a bra. The dress had two straps that tied at the base of Libby's head but her back was completely bare all the way to the top of her butt.

As he had on the dance floor, Jason slid one hand away from her face to flatten it on the small of her back, angling her body closer to his, pulling her a few inches from the wall. "Suck."

She moaned around his thick thumb and he fucked her mouth with it, letting her tongue glide around the tip and down the length, her gaze never leaving his.

Jason's eyes heated and his grip tightened, his fingers pressing against her back, slipping lower to reach a few inches below the edge of the dress. "That's so fucking hot." He stroked her butt cheek with his fingers. "Your skin is so smooth. I can't wait to run my tongue along it. You ready for that?"

She gave a garbled response around his thumb, nodding slightly.

He smiled. "You've been ready all night, haven't you, little one?"

She swallowed around his thumb as he pressed it deeper. There was no need to respond, but she shivered again when his hand slid up her back slowly until he reached the knot at the back of her neck.

He held her gaze as he easily worked the silky material loose. The moment he released the knot, the dress shimmered down her body and hit the floor, leaving her in nothing but her black lace thong and gold heels.

Her nipples puckered further than they had been all evening as the air hit them. Seconds later, Jason cupped one small breast and squeezed, his thumb and finger finding her nipple and pinching it.

She rose onto her tiptoes as the instant sting washed through her body. Her thong was soaked, and every movement caused the lace to rub against her clit.

Jason held her gaze for long seconds before lowering his face to her breast. After releasing the grip he had on her nipple, he thrummed the swollen bud with his thumb. "Gorgeous. I love how your nipples react to my touch." His thumb popped free of her mouth as he dropped to his knees in front of her.

She didn't have a moment to think before his enormous palms held her torso while his mouth descended to her nipple.

Libby gasped, her mouth falling open. She set her hands on his shoulders and then slid them into his thick, short hair. It didn't escape her attention that she was nearly naked while he was still fully clothed.

For a moment, he twirled his tongue around the swollen, tight bud, making her whimper, but then he suddenly sucked it into his mouth. Hard. Almost too hard. Just exactly hard enough.

Libby had craved an evening with a military man for years. Nothing had prepared her for this. Already she knew she was going to be ruined for other men. She'd visualized his hardness, his firm body, a thick stiff cock, but not this heady dominance. The kind of thing she thought only existed in books. The kind of thing she'd craved but never expected would happen in real life.

It snuck up on her, and she fucking loved it. If someone would have asked her an hour ago if she was submissive, she would have laughed them out of the ballroom. But the moment he'd commanded her to say goodbye to her friends, the air around them had shifted. Her usually strong, opinionated, assertive self had disappeared in a heartbeat, leaving behind someone she didn't recognize. Someone who would gladly kneel before this man and do anything he wanted.

God, this was a dream. The perfect sort of dominant. Not the cocky, macho, vain men she'd dated in the past. Not even close.

Goosebumps rose all over her skin as he stroked the underside of her other breast with his thumb. His mouth popped free, releasing the offended nipple, but only long enough to capture its twin. This time, his teeth bit down, again with the perfect pressure. Another sharp, delicious pain made her shiver.

Libby's brain could hardly keep up with Jason's movements. One second he was stroking her breasts; the next second his fingers were gripping her butt. He molded his palms to her flesh, squeezed, pulling her cheeks apart, tormenting her further with every passing second.

When he slipped his fingers under the elastic of her thong and drew it down her thighs, she moaned. He tapped one ankle and then the other to remove the skimpy garment.

This entire night was surreal. Part of her thought if she pinched herself, she would wake up and find she hadn't even attended the wedding yet. But Jason had pinched her skin so many times, that idea wasn't possible.

In another frenzied change of pace, Jason released her nipple, gripped the backs of her thighs, his palms halfway on her ass, and lifted her off the floor as he stood.

She cried out as her feet left the floor.

He was grinning at her as he flattened her to the wall, her head level with his. "Wrap your legs around me, little one."

She complied, crossing her ankles at the small of his back.

"Good girl." He spun around and carried her across the room to the bed where he deposited her on her back.

She had a tight hold around his neck, but as her body hit the mattress, he commanded, "Arms above your head, baby girl."

Libby was shaking as she released his neck and lifted her arms. She marveled at the terms of endearment he'd chosen. Coming from anyone else, they would have sounded insulting. She would have slapped any previous man who dared call her little or baby. She was self-conscious about her size most of the time. But not with Jason. Somehow it was different with him. He made her feel protected and cherished. She clasped her fingers together above her head, causing her small breasts to rise on her chest. Wetness pooled between her legs.

"Spread your legs, Libby. Wide for me, baby." He held her gaze as if taking her pulse at all times. Every ounce of his attention was on her.

This. This was what she'd been missing. A man who made it obvious he was far more interested in her needs than his own. He was bossy, but not in the way she'd previously experienced. He hadn't ordered her to take off his shoes or make him a sandwich, ensuring she was put in her place. He'd basically ordered her to...enjoy herself.

She released the grip she had with her ankles at the small of his back and opened up for him, shocked by her ability to be so easily controlled. Once again, she reminded herself how different this experience was. She'd slept with a few men. Three to be exact. None had made her burn like this. None had made her come at all.

Jason lifted off her, stood at the side of the bed, and dragged her closer to the edge. His fingers circled her ankles and then danced up her legs. "Damn, you're so fucking tiny," he murmured.

There was no arguing that point. She was petite. Every part of her. And though she'd had sex before, she was a bit concerned about how big his cock might be when and if he finally removed any of his clothes.

He trailed his fingers up her thighs and pressed them wider, making her glad she'd decided to shave—everywhere—that morning. It was unnerving lying there panting while he stared at her naked body, soaking in every inch of her, his gaze wandering up and down before landing again at the apex of her sex.

She half-thought she might orgasm before he touched her. When he parted her labia with his fingers, she gasped and arched her chest, her head tipping back at the intimacy.

Instead of touching her where she most needed contact, his fingers trailed back down her legs to her ankles. He went to work removing her dainty gold heels next.

He glanced at her, his eyes dancing with mirth. "Love these shoes. I'd leave them on, but I'm afraid you might stab me with the pointed tips while I eat your sweet pussy."

Another shiver. A rush of wetness.

He dropped the second heel to the floor and then grasped her thighs and lowered his face between her legs. With no warning or pretense, he suckled her, licking and tasting and flicking his tongue everywhere.

She cried out, gripping her fingers together, afraid she might forget his demand and lower her arms. It was hard to focus on that order, but she wasn't in the mood to find out what he might do if she disobeyed him. She wanted to know what he could do with his mouth first. And then his cock.

His lips curled around her clit, holding it captive, suckling, flicking, tormenting the tiny nub.

Her body started shaking. She whimpered as she neared orgasm quickly. This was so unlike her. She'd never come without a vibrator. She'd never come in the presence of another person. It was exhilarating. There was no way to stop it or even slow the pace.

When Jason started flicking his tongue rapidly over the bundle of nerves, she tipped over the edge, her entire body pulsing with the release as she moaned. He was relentless, not releasing her until her orgasm subsided—choosing the exact moment when the contact would have switched from glorious to too sensitive.

He lifted his face, swiped his mouth with the backs of his fingers, and then dragged her farther up the bed as if she weighed nothing. Which she did, compared to him. The man probably benched twice her weight.

Jason crawled onto the bed and up her body, nudging her legs wider before settling between them. His next frenzied assault was on her lips. The moment his mouth landed on hers, she opened for him, tasting herself on him. The sheer naughtiness of this encounter made her shudder as he angled his head to one side and devoured her.

He kissed with the same level of urgency as he'd sucked her nipples and then eaten her pussy. This first kiss was more of a tsunami. Mind-blowing. Life-altering. She was fully consumed by him. His taste. His soft lips. The power behind his every movement. The way his cock nestled between her sensitive folds as he pressed against her. Why the hell was he still dressed?

Jason cupped her face with both hands, angling her head where he wanted it. He tasted every inch of her mouth, frantically deepening the kiss with every passing moment as if he were dying of thirst and she was his last drink.

When he finally broke free, he shoved to standing again, his gaze penetrating hers as his hands went to work on the buttons of his shirt.

She lifted her arms, suddenly feeling exposed and wanting to roll to her side or shield herself in some way.

"Don't move an inch, little one," he admonished. "Keep your arms where I put them. Legs open. You're so fucking sexy. Every inch of you. Let me watch your chest rise and fall while I remove my clothes."

She sucked in a sharp breath, surprised by her willingness to obey him. It was impossible not to. He commanded it. This was his show. He was that powerful. It didn't occur to her to disobey him. It wasn't an option.

She splayed her legs open wider, pressing her knees into the mattress as she drew in deep breaths.

He dropped his dress shirt to the floor finally and slowly lifted his white T-shirt over his head. For some reason, he didn't seem to be in nearly as big of a hurry to remove his clothes. He was performing for her. Stripping. The sight was amazing.

Libby let her gaze wander down his hard, defined pecs, noticing his only tattoo was on his right bicep. She recognized the insignia as some sort of military tattoo—a skull wearing a beret with a knife between his teeth. Every inch of his skin was perfection. Gloriously masculine and all Alpha.

He undid his dress pants and lowered them next as he kicked off his shoes. Socks disappeared, and then his hands went to the waistband of his briefs to shrug them over his hips.

When his cock sprang free, she gasped before she could stop herself. He was huge. Jesus. Thick and long and so hard. His erection bobbed in front of him as he let her look. Finally, he bent over, grabbed his pants, and pulled a foil packet out of the pocket. When he stepped closer and used one knee to climb back up onto the bed, she was no longer breathing.

He nestled between her legs again, this time his warm, hard flesh pressing against her pussy. He landed on his elbows and cupped her face. "Your eyes are very wide. Are you a virgin?"

She shook her head. "No. Just... You're bigger than I've seen before."

He smiled slowly. "Don't worry. I'll work you up to it. If this is what you want, I mean. Tell me to stop and I will."

Her eyes popped wider. Stop? *Is he crazy?* "God no."

His grin widened. "Okay. Just checking. I know I'm demanding when I fuck. I like to be in control of everything, but I don't take what isn't freely offered."

"I'm yours." After those words slid out, she sucked in a breath. They were too intense for this one-night stand.

He didn't flinch though. In fact, his gaze searched her face. "I like the sound of that, little one."

She licked her lips. "For the night, I mean." *Obviously.* She didn't want him to think she was getting ahead of herself or that she was clingy. This was a one-night stand. She was clear on that.

Ignoring her explanation, he continued, "I'm going to stretch you with my fingers nice and slow, and then I'm going to fuck you. You're not going to move an inch while I do so. If you do, two things will happen." He lifted a brow.

She took the bait. "What two things are those?" Her words were barely audible. Breathy.

"I'll come too fast if you try to control things or squirm, and then I'll flip you over and spank your bottom for disobeying me before I let *you* come. Understood?" She nodded. "Yes." One word. Breathed out. The thought of his palm spanking her bottom caused a rush of arousal to run out of her. She shuddered. No one had ever come close to dominating her like this. Even verbally he was a master of her body.

In her wildest dreams, she'd never imagined this night going down like this. Him dominating her. Her obeying his every word.

Her liking it.

Craving it.

Wanting more.

Part of her wanted to feel the sting of his palm on her bottom. More of her wanted to feel his cock in her pussy.

Jason rose onto his knees and then kneeled between her legs, pressing them wider again. He held her hip down with one large hand while he found her folds with his other fingers.

He held her gaze for a long time as he eased a finger into her, and she marveled at the way he could manage to so precisely drive her mad with desire while his gaze remained on hers. And then she realized why he was doing so. He was gauging her reaction, making sure she was okay. It was endearing.

He glanced down and watched as he drew his finger in and out of her several times. "May I add a second, little one?"

"Yes. Please," she begged, instinctively trying to lift her hips.

He held her down, one brow lifting. He didn't say a word, but she felt the reprimand and stopped fighting him, forcing herself to relax into the mattress as he fingered her. "Sorry."

He gave her a knowing smile and scissored his fingers.

She moaned at the stretch. Even his two fingers were bigger than any previous cock she'd had.

"So tight, baby. Gonna add a third now."

She nodded consent, her teeth gritted against the combination of pain and pleasure he seemed fond of doling out. As he entered her, her lips parted on a gasp.

"That's it, little one. Relax. Take my fingers. My cock is smaller than how far I'm stretching you now." He pushed them deeper.

She held her breath.

When his palm flattened against her clit, she whimpered. "Such a good girl. Has anyone ever dominated you like this before, baby?"

She shook her head.

"Did you know you were submissive?"

She shook her head again.

He smiled. "You're so delightfully pliant. I've never seen anyone as deliciously submissive as you. Your obedience pleases me greatly. I will reward you."

Her body trembled.

"Are you ready for my cock, little one?"

"Yes," she breathed.

He eased his fingers out, reached for the condom, and rolled it down his length.

"I'm not a missionary kind of guy," he stated, "Not usually. But something about you makes me want to assume that position. Hover over you so I can gauge your reaction, watch your face. Your expressions are so precious." He lowered over her body again, nestling his cock at her entrance as he slid his hands up her arms and then pulled her fingers apart.

He flattened their combined hands against the mattress and kissed her again, slowly this time, as if savoring her. Without warning, he thrust into her to the hilt. She cried out at the intense pressure. The stretch. The twinge of pain.

"Relax around my cock. Let yourself adjust... That's a girl."

Her body gradually accommodated him, making her grateful he hadn't taken his time entering her. He held steady until she started to squirm with the need for friction.

He gave her a slight grin. "Don't be greedy. Stay still. I'll decide how much you get and when you get to come."

She shuddered, violently this time, his words penetrating deeply. He wasn't simply dominant; he was powerfully controlling. And damn good at it. She wondered if other women dared to defy him, and then she wondered what the consequences were like.

When she gave up the fight and settled, he finally eased almost out and then thrust back into her. For the first time, she saw a crack in his armor. His lips parted and his eyes rolled back. Before this moment, the only way she could have been sure how much she affected him had been the stiffness of his cock.

He eased back out again, seeming to gain some control, though when he met her gaze, he whispered, "You slay me. Your pussy is so fucking tight. So perfect. I'm not going to last as long as I would have liked."

How was he even able to give such a speech? Her own words were stuck somewhere, unwilling to follow the synapses of her brain to her mouth. All she could do was blink and hope he moved again soon. Harder. Faster. Anything.

It was one thing for her to have come against his mouth, but it would seem she was going to orgasm again with his cock inside her. Unexpected. All-consuming.

His eyes slid closed as he picked up the pace, pursing his

lips and gripping her hands tighter. She doubted he realized how firm his hold was. She didn't care. Her hands might be sore tomorrow. It would be worth it.

Jason's lips parted on a gasp, telling her he was close. Just when she thought he would orgasm, he stopped moving, holding his erection deep, grinding the base against her clit. "Come, baby girl. I want to feel your orgasm around my cock before I release." He pressed harder against her with his words.

She shattered, as if his command were capable of making her orgasm. Her pussy gripped at his erection, pulsing around him while her vision swam and nothing but white-hot pleasure filled her body.

Seconds later, he moved, faster, harder, deeper. And then he gasped, holding himself fully buried in her, his forehead landing on the mattress next to her face. His entire body jerked with his orgasm. She swore she could feel the pulses of his cock.

Time stood still, the earth shifting a bit on its axis as Libby fully grasped the seriousness of this situation.

She'd meant to have a one-night stand with a man in uniform. A pleasant fuck with a white guy who was tall and buff and built.

She wasn't going to see him again. He lived in Fort Hood, when he was in town. He was active military. She lived in Dallas. A flight attendant with a busy schedule and a family who would never hear of this interlude and would look down upon her with scorn if they ever found out.

She put those thoughts out of her mind. For now, she just wanted to savor this experience as long as she could. Every moment of it.

CHAPTER 2

"You just snuck out?" Christa asked as the two of them shoved their suitcases in the back of her SUV early the following morning.

"What was I supposed to do? He was dead asleep. The sun wasn't even up," Libby told her friend as she stepped out of the way so Bex and Shayla could add their overnight bags to the mix.

Shayla leaned over the suitcases to push everything to one side. Ironically, at five-eight, she was the tallest of the four of them. Ironic only because she was half-Asian. Her mother was barely taller than Libby. Her father, on the other hand, was a six-foot-two white man. Shayla was graced with a few extra inches thanks to him. She was also graced with the most gorgeous skin, hair, and eyes. They all envied her. She tucked her long, pin-straight hair behind her ear as she righted herself. "So he never even knew about your full-on walk of shame," she teased.

Bex, the quietest of them all, managed a giggle. "I still can't believe you had sex with a man you met twenty-four hours earlier. I'd never have balls that big."

Libby shrugged, glancing at the front of the hotel. She wanted the four of them to pull away before Jason woke up and found her gone. She half-expected him to come out the front door any second, looking for her.

As soon as they were all situated inside the SUV, Christa driving, Libby in the front passenger seat, Bex and Shayla behind her, Libby blew out a sigh of relief.

"Why do I get the feeling you're in a rush to escape?" Christa asked as she pulled out of the parking lot.

"Not escape, really. Just... I don't know what I'm doing." Libby wasn't kidding. She was still trembling from everything that had happened, not even close to processing her feelings. Unexpected was all she could come up with so far.

"He seemed incredibly nice and totally into you. Did he suck between the sheets?" Christa asked.

Libby laughed. "God no. Best sex of my life, hands down. I'm seriously ruined for all other men."

"And how is this a problem?" Bex asked.

"I'm worried about shaking him from my mind is all."

Shayla grabbed Libby's seat from behind. "Why do you have to?"

Libby sighed as she closed her eyes and leaned her head back. "You know how my parents are. My mom would have a stroke if she found out I wasted my time even dancing with Jason. If she thought I had feelings for him, she would drop dead on the spot."

"You have feelings for him?" Bex's voice rose.

Libby shook her head. "No. Of course not. I mean...no. It was good sex. That's all. How could I have feelings for a man I exchanged less than a dozen words with? It was nothing more than a one-night stand. I'm sure he would agree."

Christa glanced at Libby. "Did you ask him?"

Libby shook her head. "We seriously didn't discuss a single thing. We had amazing sex and then he held me in his arms. I couldn't even fall asleep for the longest time." It took her over an hour just to calm her racing heart. "But he's military. Probably travels more than he's home. And I live two hours away in Dallas. I also travel more than I don't. It's not like I could have made plans to see him again later this week. I'm scheduled to work the next four days in a row."

"Aren't we all," Shayla groaned. "Taking these two days off all at the same time was an amazing feat in and of itself."

Christa ignored Shayla, her focus on Libby. "That sure was a long list of excuses. I mean, I know how your parents feel about you dating men who aren't specifically from Guatemala, but you can't cater to them your entire life. At some point, you have to stick up for yourself and do whatever makes you happy. If you like this Jason guy, go out with him again. See where it leads."

Libby nodded. "I'll think about it." She turned her gaze to stare out the window as they sped down the highway. She wouldn't think about it. Not for a moment. Everything about what happened last night needed to be erased from her mind.

Besides the distance, their busy work schedules, and her parents' inevitable disapproval, Jason had awoken something in her she wasn't willing to face.

Sure, she'd read erotic romance novels. She'd looked up anything she didn't understand on the internet. She grasped the concept of BDSM. It appealed to her on a visceral level. However, she'd never considered herself submissive. That didn't suit her at all. She'd always thought she was the polar opposite of submissive. She was a strong, independent woman. She'd worked her ass off to put herself through school and then flight attendant training. She was still pretty low on the totem pole with the airline, but she intended to climb up in the ranks. She was assertive and a good leader.

Not submissive.

Right?

Last night had caused her to doubt herself. Who did that sort of thing? What possessed her to permit Jason to order her around, force her to keep her hands in one spot and not squirm? She squirmed a bit now at the memory. Order her to come when he was ready? Threaten to *spank* her?

Lord, she was out of her mind. She felt raw and vulnerable this morning. Out of control. It had been too intense. She couldn't let something like that happen again. Not with him. Not with anyone.

CHAPTER 3

"She snuck out? You didn't even notice?" Kraft, whose real name was Mack Carter, cringed as he took a giant bite of pancakes. Kraft had rightfully earned his nickname as soon as their Delta team formed. The man's favorite food, which he ate several times a week, was boxed mac and cheese. At least this morning he was having pancakes. Though Jason doubted the hotel restaurant served mac and cheese at this hour. "Hatch, dude, that's brutal. When was the last time a lady snuck out of your bed?"

Jason groaned after setting his coffee cup down. He wasn't hungry. His omelet was still untouched in front of him. "No woman has ever had the *opportunity* to sneak out of my bed."

Kraft chuckled. "For real? No one?" He shoveled another giant mouthful of syrupy pancakes in and chewed.

"Nope. I don't bring women back to my place. I go to theirs. If there's any sneaking, it's me." Jason was scowling. He knew it. He couldn't stop it. He was in a foul mood. The only reason he'd packed up his suitcase and come downstairs to meet up with Kraft was because he'd made that arrangement earlier in the day yesterday. They would meet for breakfast and then head back to base.

That was before. Before Jason knew he wouldn't feel like eating breakfast. Before he'd hooked up with Libby. Before she'd rocked his world in his hotel room. Before she'd slipped out of his room while he slept.

When he'd woken up, he'd bolted to sitting, knowing instantly she was no longer in the room. Her scent lingered. The floral smell of her shampoo was on the pillow. The bed was still warm next to him. Other than that, not a trace.

Why?

Jason had dropped onto his back and stared at the ceiling. He'd just had the best fucking night of his life and the woman he'd shared it with was gone. Had he said or done something to make her flee like that?

And why the hell did he care? He hadn't brought her to his room last night with the intention of anything more than a one-night stand. He felt confident she'd returned the sentiment. They'd flirted. Danced. Fucked.

Except it hadn't been a simple fuck like he'd expected. It had been far more. He hadn't known she would be submissive. He hadn't considered the possibility that he might dominate her. Not until he had her in his arms on the dance floor. Not until he instructed her to tell her friends goodbye.

He still wasn't sure what possessed him to test her like that. But the moment the words were out of his mouth, her heart rate picked up and she sucked in a breath, her gaze holding his while she licked her lips and shivered.

His cock had gone rock hard, and the situation had escalated from there. Small talk had flown out the window when he'd flattened her to the wall in his room and started removing her clothes. Emboldened by her reactions, he hadn't stopped there. He'd continued adding to his demands. She'd obeyed his every word.

Jason had never dominated a woman who wasn't already in the lifestyle and with whom he hadn't negotiated before having sex with her. There were two possibilities where Libby was concerned. Either she was familiar with dominance and submission and therefore fell into step. Or—and he was inclined to believe this latter option—she'd been just as shocked by her reactions as him.

Either way, she'd rocked his world unexpectedly. And now she was gone.

"So, you gonna call her?"

Jason shook his head. "Ball's not in my court. She's the one who left without a word. If she wants to see me again, she can call me."

"Did you at least exchange phone numbers?"

"Nope. But obviously, she knows people who could get her my information."

Kraft leaned back in his chair and sighed, holding Jason's gaze. After a few moments, he rubbed his forehead with two fingers. "Gotta be honest with you, Hatch."

"What?" Jason sat up straighter.

"I don't think she'll call. If she was that good and you want to see her again, you'll have to hunt her down."

"What makes you say that?" Hunting women down was not something Jason ever did. If a woman wanted to go out with him, she needed to put herself out there. He wasn't about to turn into some pansy and go after a woman who snuck out of his hotel room without a word. No matter how good a lay she was.

Kraft sighed. "I overheard her friends talking after you two left last night. I was in the men's room. The other women were a bit tipsy and probably didn't realize they were kind of loud outside the women's bathroom."

Jason could picture Libby's friends. Her posse of flight

attendants. All friends of the bride, Destiny, who was also a flight attendant for Open Skies. "What did they say?"

"First of all, mostly they were jealous. They thought you were smokin' hot—their words, not mine—and they fully supported Libby's choice."

Jason narrowed his gaze. "How is this a bad thing?"

Kraft cringed. "They also laughed about her choice to pursue a one-night stand with a man in uniform. Apparently, Libby's plan was to get between the sheets with a military man. Her girls were hoping she knew what she was doing and didn't end up falling for you because it wasn't her goal."

Jason blew out a breath and turned his gaze toward the window at his right, staring out at nothing. He couldn't really be angry. When he'd lured Libby upstairs last night, he'd had nothing on his mind but a fuck, too. She didn't even live nearby. She was from Dallas, more than two hours away. She had a busy schedule. So did he. Pursuing her beyond last night hadn't been on his radar.

Not until he'd had her.

No. Even that wasn't true. He'd known she was special far earlier than that. Within moments of pulling her into his arms on the dance floor, he'd felt the spark. She'd gone from just a pretty girl flirting with him to a sexy woman whose gaze locked on his and didn't let go.

"Maybe she's just a base bunny." Kraft shrugged. "Sure sounded like it. She can now say she's bedded a soldier."

Jason cringed and shook his head. "No way. Not Libby." *Right?* Was there merit to what Kraft was suggesting? Jason certainly wouldn't have cared one way or the other before they'd headed upstairs. But now... Jesus. He shuddered. He wasn't willing to entertain that possibility.

Nope. What he'd shared with Libby last night had not been superficial. Even if she'd intended it to be. It hadn't remained that way.

His uncontrolled feelings had clenched when he'd issued his first demand and she'd reacted with a shudder instead of slapping him.

By the time he'd had her naked underneath him, his face buried in her pussy, her fucking sweet taste on his tongue, he'd been a goner for her.

The joke was on him apparently. She was the one who was gone before dawn. He couldn't blame her. They hadn't discussed a single detail about future plans. Hell, they hadn't exchanged many words at all. What did he expect? That she would wake up in the morning, smile at him, and agree to be his girlfriend?

What a joke. Jason didn't do girlfriends. He didn't have time for them. When he got out of the Army, maybe then he would think about finding a woman to spend his nights with, but until then he wouldn't even consider a relationship with any permanence.

He cringed as he recalled the one and only serious relationship he'd ever been in. It had been three years since he and Veronica broke up, and it still smarted. He'd never let himself get involved with a woman like that again.

He knew nothing about Libby really, other than the fact that the two of them were incredibly compatible in bed. She didn't seem like someone who would treat people the way Veronica did, but how much did Jason really know about Libby?

He took a deep breath and shook the thoughts of last night from his head. He was a fool to mope. He needed to eat this damn omelet and get on the road.

Libertad Garcia was cute and all, but he didn't know her well enough to let her take up space in his head. At least that's what he chose to tell himself.

CHAPTER 4

Six months later…

He felt her presence even before he saw her. It didn't matter that it was illogical. No one could possibly sense a woman he hadn't seen in six months and spin around to find her standing behind him. But that's exactly what happened.

Granted, there were other factors. Like the smell of her shampoo maybe, or the distinct tone of her laughter.

In any case, Jason found himself face-to-face with Libby in the middle of a crowded bar in Dallas. For several seconds, he stared at her. She looked fucking amazing. Her long, nearly black hair hung in thick waves down her back. She hadn't cut it since he'd last threaded his fingers in those silky locks. She was wearing a killer black dress that hugged her curves perfectly. And that same sexy pair of gold heels was on her dainty feet, making her stand all of about five-three, tops. Even with the heels, she was nearly a foot shorter than him.

"Hey," she breathed out, licking those soft lips, the ones he remembered as if he'd tasted them yesterday instead of months ago.

"Hey yourself," he replied, feeling like a moron. Of course, that was the exact moment his date wrapped her fingers around his arm, reminding him of her existence. Her bleach blond hair dangled over his arm. Her fake tanned fingers gripped his biceps.

Jason didn't even spare her a glance. He didn't even care if he was being rude. His gaze was locked on Libby until it slid to the man who set a possessive hand on the small of her back.

Jason's reaction to Libby was completely unexpected. He thought he'd finally purged her from his head. Apparently not, because now all he could think about was the feel of her skin beneath his palm when he'd danced with her at the wedding. She'd been wearing a backless dress, affording him the luxury of enjoying her smooth skin.

She was the one to finally break the spell, physically shaking out of their trance. She shifted her attention to the man at her side. The guy seemed younger than her. Maybe twenty-five. He had the same dark skin as Libby and black hair.

Libby spoke. "Eduardo, this is Jason. I met him at my friend Destiny's wedding a while back."

Eduardo reached out a hand. "Eddie. Nice to meet you."

Jason took the man's hand, noticing his firm grip. He wasn't as tall as Jason, but he pulled his shoulders back and pumped out his chest. He was wearing a deep purple silk shirt, the top three buttons undone.

"Oh, how fun. What are the chances we would run into friends of yours?" Tiffany said at Jason's side. She stuck out a hand next, her hot pink manicure catching his eye. Libby didn't have fake nails. He would remember. After all, she'd dug those nails into his biceps when he'd finally let her move them from above her head. Libby didn't have fake anything.

Her skin was the same shade over every inch of her body, including her amazing ass and tits. Her hair wasn't dyed or permed either. It was soft as silk. And her small breasts were just the right handful, not filled with silicone.

"I'm Tiffany," his fake date said.

Libby shook her hand politely, her smile forced. Jason wondered what she thought of his date. The only thing the two of them had in common was they both spoke English. And even that comparison was bad since Jason figured Libby also spoke perfect Spanish.

"What are you doing in Dallas?" Libby asked.

"I moved here about a month ago."

Libby's eyes widened and she licked her lips in a way that made him want to yank her out of Eddie's grip and pull her against his chest to remind her what she craved. "Oh." Her lips were still parted like she wanted to continue speaking, but she glanced at Eddie and then Tiffany and closed her mouth.

Jason couldn't know exactly what she was thinking, but he agreed with her on one thing. He didn't want to share any conversation he might have with her in front of anyone else. He wished Tiffany and Eddie would disappear.

Jason was seriously fucked-up. He thought he'd finally gotten Libby out of his mind and here she was, dragging every detail back to the forefront. His imagination wandered to visions of her lying beneath him. The way her small body accepted his cock. How her gorgeous hair spread out on his pillow. How she writhed beneath him when he made her come.

The bar was crowded. It hadn't been Jason's first choice of places to go this evening, but Tiffany had suggested it. She'd wanted to go dancing. Oddly enough, though they'd been here for half an hour and had been heading to the bar behind Libby to get another drink, they had yet to dance. Jason wasn't feeling it. At least not with Tiffany. Libby on the other hand…

Shit. He would pull her onto the dance floor without any coaxing. And he had. Six months ago.

Someone bumped into Libby from behind. While Eddie spun around to grab the drunk guy by the shoulders, Libby stumbled forward. She reached out to keep from falling, her palm landing on Jason's chest. She hesitated for several heartbeats before slowly removing her hand. "Sorry."

He reached out to squeeze her fingers as she withdrew, releasing her reluctantly after a second. "Not your fault. It's crowded in here." It was also loud. The only reason they could hear each other was because they were a ways away from the dance floor.

Eddie, however, wasn't as calm. He snarled at the man who'd bumped into Libby before turning back to face her, his brow furrowed, shoulders back again. A tough guy. "You okay?" Eddie asked.

Jason couldn't decide if the guy was trying to impress Libby, or if he had a temper.

"Yeah. I'm fine." Libby replied.

"We were about to grab a table, if you want to join us," Tiffany suggested.

Jason stiffened. The last thing he wanted to do was awkwardly try to make small talk with Libby's date. He'd had his mouth on her pussy. He'd tasted her. Swallowed her moans when she came. Had Eddie?

It was kind of Tiffany to make the suggestion, however. He certainly couldn't complain about her as a person. She was gorgeous and fun and apparently extremely polite. As blind dates went, he'd done well. Until he'd been reminded that she wasn't Libby.

Libby opened her mouth as if to respond to Tiffany's suggestion, but Eddie cut her off. "We're with other friends, actually. Maybe some other time." He set a palm on Libby's lower back and turned as if to steer her away.

Libby chewed on her bottom lip, not glancing at Eddie, but not making eye contact with Jason either. Her gaze seemed to wander up and down his torso. Was she remembering his naked body the way he was remembering hers? The world stopped spinning for several heartbeats.

The music changed to a slow song at that moment. Tiffany's face lit up. "Finally. A slow song. Will you dance with me *now*?"

"I thought we were going to get a drink," he pointed out, nodding toward the bar, his gaze still flicking to Libby every few seconds.

Damn, she looked good.

Tiffany shrugged. "That was before the music changed. Let's dance first. We can get a drink after."

For a heartbeat, Jason considered telling Tiffany to fuck off. But he wasn't that kind of guy. By the end of this night, she was undoubtedly going to want to throttle him, but he wasn't willing to tip that boat just yet. He would be a total dick if he ditched her.

Besides, there were no guarantees Libby would even speak to him further, let alone behave rudely to her date. "Nice seeing you. Enjoy your evening," she said, her gaze on his far longer than necessary.

"So nice meeting you guys," Tiffany added.

Jason's heart was pounding as he watched Libby disappear, another man's hand on the small of her back. Jason had to force himself to turn and walk away. It was the last thing he wanted to do. But it was necessary.

When he and Tiffany reached the dance floor, she set her hands on Jason's waist and stepped closer. He planted his palms on her back but made no effort to draw her against him.

Apparently, Tiffany wasn't daunted by Jason running into Libby. She didn't mention it. Instead, she started making small talk again. Perfectly normal. After all, they'd just met a few hours ago.

Honestly, Tiffany was a nice enough woman. He couldn't really complain about her. She wasn't stereotypically ditzy or anything. She worked for a bank. She was pretty. He supposed most men would give anything for a date with her. But his mind was on Libby now, and nothing was going to change that development.

It was simply bad luck for Tiffany that Jason had his eyes on another woman. One of his coworkers had set them up. The truth was, he'd only agreed because he hadn't been on a date in months. He'd been on several missions in a row with his Delta Team, and then he'd dealt with leaving the team and moving to Dallas.

"...and then my girlfriend, Jazmine, she thought it would be funny if we went skinny dipping." Tiffany giggled. "The water was so cold. My nipples were hard for hours."

Jason offered her a smile. She was flirting with him. Heavily. She kept patting his chest and leaning in closer than necessary to speak. When her hair brushed against his cheek, he was shocked to find that it was kind of stiff. Like it had received far too many treatments and had a lot of hairspray in it.

As the song wound down, Jason spotted Libby over Tiffany's shoulder. She was heading toward the hallway where the restrooms were located. She was also alone.

Jason jerked his attention back to Tiffany and then nodded toward the far wall. "Why don't you find us a high-top table over there? I'm going to use the restroom, and then I'll get us some drinks."

She nodded. "Okay. Sure."

As soon as she walked away, Jason hurried toward the corner where Libby had disappeared. He got lucky. She was just exiting the women's room as he approached. She lifted her gaze and smiled.

That was all the encouragement he needed to grab her hand and pull her farther down the hallway toward the rear exit. He shoved the door open and stepped out into the night, keeping her close.

She looked over her shoulder as the door closed behind them. "Jason, what are you doing? I can't just leave."

He flattened her against the brick wall and cupped her face, angling her head so he could see her eyes. "We're not leaving. I just wanted a moment."

"Okay," she whispered breathlessly before glancing around.

No one else was standing nearby. Certainly not Eddie, who undoubtedly thought she was in the bathroom.

"You snuck out of my bed," he began.

She licked her lips. "I thought it would be easier than dealing with the morning-after chat and a pile of empty, fake promises to call or something."

He slid his hand around to cup her neck, his fingers threading in her hair. "I would have called."

She sucked in a breath. "Yeah?"

He frowned. "Why would you doubt that? What part of the evening suggested I wasn't into you?" He reminded her by setting his other hand on her waist and then sliding it up just far enough to let his thumb graze the underside of her breast.

Her breath hitched again, and she rose up slightly on her toes.

"You were into me too, baby girl," he whispered, leaning in close to her ear. He loved the way she shivered. "Tell me I'm wrong." He stepped closer, flattening his chest to hers, his thumb still grazing her breast. "Tell me you're not still into me and I'll walk away right now."

She whimpered. "Jason..." His name on her lips was ambrosia.

When she didn't deny the truth he spoke, he finally pulled back enough to meet her gaze again. "I could slide my hand down over your sweet bottom, reach under your skirt, and bring you to orgasm right here against the wall in seconds, couldn't I?"

She nodded, biting her lip.

"How wet are you, little one?"

She swallowed. God, he loved her expressions. "Soaked," she whispered.

He leaned in slowly, kissed her neck gently, and then released her. "Here's what's gonna happen. You're going to take off your panties right here and give them to me. Then you're going to go back inside and continue your evening. I'll continue mine. Tomorrow, you'll contact me. Do it before noon."

She gasped and glanced around.

"No one's looking, and you won't be the first woman to remove her panties in public. I trust you can do so discreetly." He lifted a brow.

For a heartbeat, she simply stared at him. Finally, she glanced around again and then lifted the edges of her short tight black dress and dragged a black thong over her hips and down her legs. She stepped out of the lace quickly and balled it in her fist before handing it to him.

Jason's cock was fucking hard as a rock from watching, but more importantly from witnessing her submission. He took the black lace and brought it to his nose, inhaling her amazing scent. The material was indeed soaked.

Finally, he tucked them in his jeans pocket and met her gaze again.

She was stunned and biting into her bottom lip. "Next

time I tell you to do something, you won't hesitate, understood?"

"Yes," she breathed. God, she was fucking delightful.

"You can go back inside now."

She righted herself, pushing off the wall that had been supporting her. As she started to turn toward the door, he reached out and grabbed her hand.

"One more thing. Do not have sex with Eddie tonight."

She shivered, her voice soft. "Wasn't planning on it."

"Good." He released her and nodded toward the door. "Have fun."

"Fat chance of that," she murmured as she stepped back inside.

Jason stood there for several moments, smiling far too wide to return to Tiffany yet. He would give her the wrong impression if he didn't get his emotions under control. There wasn't a chance in hell he would sleep with her either, but that wasn't important right now. He needed to politely get them new drinks and then make some excuses about not being that into her and wrap this evening up. Tiffany was already in his past.

CHAPTER 5

"Are you serious?" Destiny asked, her voice squealing through the phone the next morning. "Christa told me you hooked up with Hatch at the wedding but I thought it was a one-night stand kind of thing."

Libby cringed. She hated having to call Destiny to get Jason's phone number. He'd obviously intended for her to work for it when he ordered her to contact him before noon. She'd had no choice but to call Destiny who would have to speak to Trent, ensuring both of them shared this interesting gossip with the rest of their friends, male and female.

"Libby? You still there?"

"Yeah. It was. A one-night stand, I mean. For me at least. He was hot. I was horny. I thought it was understood."

"And now?"

Libby sighed. "I don't know. The man gets way under my skin. He makes my brain go to mush when I'm with him." She wasn't about to tell Destiny the specifics. Way too much information. If any of her friends found out what sort of dynamic Libby had with Jason, she would be beyond embarrassed.

Destiny laughed. "Good. That's new for you. You're usually too stiff and in control of everything. I like hearing someone rattles your mind a bit."

"I've got to be crazy calling him. It's a bad idea." She'd paced her apartment all morning before giving in and calling Destiny. She'd gone back and forth, trying to decide if it was wise to follow through with Jason's demands. Undoubtedly she should have shrugged him off and continued with her life. She'd almost changed into workout clothes and gone for a run to pass the time until after noon.

But in the end, she hadn't been able to resist the pull. The curiosity. The excitement. She'd been aroused since the moment she first saw him last night. When she'd finally managed to extricate herself from her mother's latest attempt to set her up last night, she'd gone home, stripped, and grabbed her vibrator. It took two drawn-out orgasms before she could relax enough to fall asleep, and even then she'd woken up several hours later after an erotic dream about Jason, panting and squirming under her sheets.

"I don't see why you're so reluctant. Hatch is a good guy. Trent vouches for him. How can you go wrong?"

Libby sighed. "You know perfectly well how this would go over with my mom. She'd have a conniption."

"Yeah, but you can't live under her thumb, Libby. You're twenty-eight years old. How long do you plan to go out with every Guatemalan man in Dallas that your mom sets you up with?"

Intellectually, Destiny was right. Libby knew it. But she'd never had the balls to confront her mom. Instead, she politely put up with the woman's antics. Ironic, considering the fact that Libby wasn't such a pushover in the rest of her life. She couldn't afford to be. She'd been the smallest one in any room for her entire life. She'd made up for her stature with her personality, ensuring people at school and work and even in her personal life knew she was a strong, independent woman.

If she couldn't reach something, she got a ladder. If she didn't know something, she looked it up. If she felt emotions welling, she waited until she was alone to let the tears fall.

Except with Jason. That man controlled her with ease. It was both unnerving and intriguing.

"I figure eventually I'll meet someone my mom approves of that I also like." This was true. It was why she rarely turned down all the arranged dates. Surely one of these days the right man would show up at her door and she'd fall for him.

"*Like?* Do you hear yourself? You aren't looking for a man you *like*, Libby. You need to find someone you're head over heels in love with. No exceptions."

Libby chuckled. "Just because you met that man when you were five, doesn't mean the same thing happens for the rest of us. Besides, you got lucky that you finally ran into him after more than a decade of misunderstandings and cleared the air with your tequila mouth."

Destiny laughed. "I was pretty drunk that night. Thank God. But seriously, you must at least like Jason more than any recent guy you've dated or you wouldn't have gone to the trouble to call and get his number," she pointed out.

She was right. Libby took in a deep breath. "What's he doing in Dallas? Do you know? He said he moved here."

"He got out of the Army a few months ago. He got a job here."

"Oh. I didn't realize that." She hadn't taken the time to ask him any questions last night.

Destiny giggled. "You two don't do much talking, do you?"

Libby flushed. Destiny was right. *How embarrassing.*

"Hey," Destiny whispered before going silent for several seconds.

Libby could hear her shuffling around.

"Sorry. I wanted to step outside so Trent wouldn't hear me."

Libby frowned. "Since when do you keep secrets from Trent?"

"Never. This isn't something he doesn't know. I just didn't want him to realize I was telling you."

"Oh." Libby stiffened.

"Maybe you already figured this out but just in case you didn't, Jason is, uh, kind of, well, dominant."

Libby closed her eyes, shocked and uncertain what she wanted to divulge.

Destiny continued, rambling. "I mean it's more than that. He's a Dom, Libby. Do you know what that is?"

Libby nearly choked. "Yes, Mom. I'm not that innocent. I've read books. I have the internet."

"Oh. Right. Sorry. Well... I just thought you should know. If he's pursuing you, you'll eventually find that out, I guess, but maybe if I warned you..."

"Destiny, stop. I'm aware." It felt weird admitting this to one of her closest friends, but it also felt like a weight had been lifted. At least she would have someone she could talk to if she had questions or concerns.

"You are?"

"Yes. He doesn't exactly hide that fact and save it for the second or third date."

"Oh. Wow. Okay. Hmm. Then I guess you, uh..."

"I'm not ready to discuss it with you, okay? It's kinda weird and personal and I'm still wrapping my head around it."

"Okay. Sure. I get it. It's not like I'm well-versed in any sort of kink anyway. I'm just, well, I'm here for you if you need to talk."

"Thank you. That means a lot. Really. I appreciate it, and thanks for looking out for me, even though you're a date-and-a-half too late," Libby joked, chuckling. "Now, text me his number so I can call him before he gets his panties in a wad. As you obviously know, the man doesn't like to be challenged."

"Got it. Good luck. Be careful."

"Be careful? You just went to a great deal of trouble pointing out he was a good guy and I was in good hands," Libby teased.

"He is. I meant with your heart."

Libby flinched. Destiny was right. There was little concern for her physical wellbeing. Her heart was another story.

The moment Libby ended the call, there was a knock at the door. She shuffled over and opened it to find a teenager holding a narrow vase with a single rose in it. "Delivery for Libertad Garcia."

She smiled as she took it from him. Apparently, even though she hadn't tracked Jason down until just now, he'd found her information. The man had been busy this morning. Impressive.

As she shut the door, she leaned in and inhaled the scent. It wasn't until she'd carried the rose over to set it on the counter that she noticed there was no card. Nothing. Just the rose.

So, the man was romantic and mysterious.

And dominant, she reminded herself.

CHAPTER 6

Jason smiled when his phone indicated there was an incoming text. His little imp had kept him waiting. It was five minutes until noon. He wasn't surprised. He'd expected as much.

He took a deep, cleansing breath and dropped onto his couch, keeping the face of his phone against his jeans for a few more seconds. He needed to get himself under control. He'd never been this interested in a woman before. He didn't want to fuck it up.

Finally, he lifted his phone to read her text.

Reporting in as demanded before noon, Sir.

He nearly swallowed his tongue. His cock jumped to attention. *Holy shit.* She'd even called him Sir. It wasn't a term he had ever demanded from a submissive, but he liked the sound of it. Except for her tone, which he could easily discern. He smiled as he responded.

What a sassy little girl. Do you have any idea what happens to sassy girls?

He waited, wiping his palm on his jeans, his other hand shaking. How the fuck had this little imp gotten under his skin? He wanted her so badly he was chomping at the bit.

Finally, a response.

No... But I'm sure you'll inform me.

He smiled again as he typed.

Count on it. I'll demonstrate in fact. With my palm. Tonight. I'll text you my address. Be here at seven.

He knew he was being presumptuous. He also gambled that she would not turn him down. He'd bet his last dollar she would rearrange any plans she might have had to get to him.

Cocky. What if I'm not available tonight?

Make yourself available. Seven. Sharp. See you then. Oh, and baby girl, if you wear panties to my house, you won't see them again.

He followed that text with his address, guessing she wouldn't respond.

She didn't.

Now he just needed to occupy his time for the next seven hours so he wouldn't lose his mind waiting for Libby to arrive.

CHAPTER 7

What the hell was she thinking? Libby was decidedly out of her mind. Showing up at Jason's door this evening had to have been the most hairbrained idea of her life.

Sure, she'd had a one-night stand. Yes, it had been the best sex of her life, hands down. Yes, she realized she would never experience anything even close to that again. Still…returning for more was ludicrous. She already knew based on her reaction to Jason the night in his hotel room and last night outside the bar that she would melt the moment he opened the door. He brought out something in her she hadn't known existed. It both scared her and exhilarated her.

She stood on his front porch for several moments, wringing her hands together while she stared at the door. She was still working up the nerve to knock when the door opened. Of course. He easily could have seen or heard her pull into his driveway and exit her Honda.

She sucked in a breath at his appearance. The only thing he was wearing was a pair of jeans. No shirt. No shoes. No socks. Just the jeans. Her mouth watered, and she licked her lips.

He leaned his shoulder against the door frame and crossed his arms loosely, smirking. "I wasn't sure if you were going to knock or just stand out here."

"Sorry. I was working up to it." Her gaze roamed to his chest. His damn fine chest. He was living sculpture with muscles upon muscles. She wanted to flatten her palms on his pecs. Hell, she wanted to drag her tongue across them.

"Are you afraid of me?"

She jerked her gaze upward and shook her head. "No. I'm afraid of *me*." That was the truth. For some reason she trusted him. Maybe because he'd given her no indication he would harm her or anyone. Maybe because Destiny knew him, and surely Trent wouldn't let a friend of his wife get involved with a known ax murderer.

He smiled. "I can work with that." And then he held out a hand, giving her the power to choose to take it or not.

She took a deep breath and then reached out and set her much smaller hand in his.

"That's my girl." He pulled her against him, trapping her palm against his chest while his free hand threaded in her hair and tugged hard enough to get her to tip her head back. "That denim has to be chafing against your clit, little one."

She stopped breathing. It was. But the fact that it was the first thing he pointed out was shocking. "Yes."

"Do you like that? Did you get off from it?"

She squirmed as much as she could in his firm grip. They were still standing in the open doorway, and she wondered when he might back up and invite her inside. A tiny voice in the back of her head warned her that a neighbor might be watching this interaction. Though really, to a distant eye it would just look like two lovers drawn into an embrace.

"No." She hadn't. She had considered it, but she hadn't touched herself all day either. She'd wanted to let the arousal build before she got here.

He lifted a brow. "Impressive. Did you masturbate today?"

"No." She felt her face heat.

"Last night?"

"Yes." That one word was breathy. "Twice." No sense lying to him. He'd insisted she not have sex with Eddie—and there had never been any chance of that happening—but he hadn't said a word about masturbating.

He tipped her chin back farther and gently kissed her lips before stepping back just enough to shut the door. Before she had a chance to look around, he flattened her to the door and cupped her face, blocking her view of the inside of his home. "Did you let Eddie touch you?"

Ah. So he intended to continue this line of questioning.

She shuddered at the thought. "No. And I wouldn't have, even if I hadn't run into you. I wasn't into him."

"Why were you out with him?"

"My mother set me up," she confessed.

"Your mom?" His eyes crinkled with humor.

"Yeah. Long story."

"Can't wait to hear it. But back to your hot body. Did you get yourself off with your fingers or did you use a toy?"

She swallowed. He was demanding such personal information from her. And she felt compelled to answer every question. "A vibrator. I've never been able to come without a vibrator."

He lifted a brow. "You came with me after the wedding. I didn't use a vibrator."

She stared at him.

Both brows lifted. "Have you never orgasmed with a man?"

She shook her head. "You're about to go all kinds of cocky on me now, aren't you?"

"Yes. *Hell*, yes." He smiled as he released her hand and slid his fingers up to touch her chin.

She flattened her palm on his chest and enjoyed the sheer power he exuded. The warmth of his smooth, hard skin.

Finally, he released his grip on her hair and slid his fingers down her arms to clasp her hands in his as he stepped back. "Come on. I'll show you around and then we can talk. I realized I know very little about you except that you're an amazing submissive, and my cock gets all kinds of hard every time I'm around you because of it."

"I'm not a submissive really."

He gave her another slow smile. "Is that so?"

She drew in a breath. "I mean, I never thought about it. I've never been with anyone like you. I've read about it of course, but never considered something like that for me in real life."

"But you've fantasized."

She shrugged. "Hasn't everyone?"

"I have no idea, but I'm not complaining. You're so pure. It's hot."

It was hot all right. Her face was burning from the level of intimate conversation they'd already engaged in, and she'd been here all of five minutes. "Yeah, well, you should know I have no idea what you might be expecting of me. I'll probably fuck it up."

He chuckled. "For right now, I expect you to talk to me while I feed you. We'll see how things go after that. I don't follow some sort of protocol. It's more of a natural thing. I'll take my cues from you and do my best to meet your needs."

"My needs?"

"Yep. That's what it's all about, really. Dominance and submission, I mean. I love nothing more than fulfilling a woman's every desire." He tapped her nose. "And you, little one, get off on having a firm hand in control. So, if we move to my bedroom later, then I'll expect you to submit to me. But for right now, I want you to relax and tell me everything there is to know about Libertad Garcia."

She smiled at him. "Your Spanish accent is amazing."

"I learned it in the Army. Part of the job. Language immersion. I'm not the best, but I can get by." He tugged her hand as he turned toward the room.

She was shocked to find it empty. "You, uh, lack furniture."

He laughed. "Yep. Just bought this place a month ago. I haven't had a chance to fully furnish it. I've been working a lot, so I had to choose one room at a time on the weekends. I started with the master bedroom and then moved to the office. One of these days maybe I'll add a couch," he joked.

"Destiny told me you got out of the Army recently."

"Yes. I was tired. It was time." He slowly led her through his empty living room and into his kitchen on the other side. This room lacked a table and regular chairs, but it at least had an island and two bar stools. "And here we have my equally unfurnished kitchen." He swung an arm around. The room smelled of pizza and there were two boxes on the island.

Libby liked the house. It was a new build in a new neighborhood, so the walls were standard builder off-white. The carpet in the living room was beige. The kitchen echoed with every word from the lack of furniture. The cabinets were a dark brown, and the island and counters were a brown speckled granite.

"I hope you like pizza," he said as he lured her closer and pulled out a barstool.

"Are there people who don't like pizza?" she inhaled the delicious scent, surprised she could manage an appetite amid the sexual tension she'd experienced all day that had only intensified since her arrival.

He shrugged. "I haven't met any, and I'd probably be seriously concerned about you if you told me you hated it."

"I'm safe for now then." She smiled up at him. Even though she was now seated higher than her normal short self on the stool, he was still towering over her. "You might be seriously concerned about me for any number of reasons after you get to know me, but I do pass the pizza test."

"Good." He slid the top box next to the bottom box and lifted both lids. "That brings us to the next question. Are you picky or easy to please?" He lifted a brow and nodded toward the two pizzas. One was cheese only. The other was supreme.

"Since you worded it that way, I'd say I pass pizza test number two. I'm not fond of anchovies or pineapple, but everything else is delicious."

"Excellent." He closed the lid on the cheese pizza and spun around to stick it in the fridge.

"You bought two pizzas just in case I didn't like the toppings?" *Impressive.*

"Yep. It won't go to waste. I'll add a bunch of stuff to it tomorrow and pop it in the oven." He grabbed plates from the cabinet and then returned to the fridge for a handful of sodas. "I wasn't sure what you liked." He set a cola, an orange, a root beer, and a lemon-lime on the island.

"Did you also buy all these with me in mind?"

"Yep."

"That's so...thoughtful. Thank you." She reached for the root beer.

"Normally, I would offer you wine or beer or a mixed drink, but the first night we were together we'd had a few drinks, and last night you'd been drinking too. Tonight, I thought we'd be ourselves. Is that okay?"

"Of course." This entire scene was so domestic. Like a regular date. She wasn't sure what she'd expected, but since her only interactions with Jason had been sexual, part of her thought he might strip her naked the moment she arrived and have her on her knees sucking him off before saying a word.

That scenario was oddly not unwelcome either. She'd visualized it many times since the night they met. She'd probably exaggerated what their dynamic might be if they ever fucked again. Her fantasies had gotten carried away. But the thought of giving this giant of a man a blow job under his command had been the fodder of many of her daydreams. Most of them, in fact.

She shuddered.

Jason was standing on the other side of the island still, but he reached across and clasped her hand in his. When she lifted her gaze, he was smiling at her warmly. "I'm not going to ask what you were just thinking, but it must have been amazing."

She flinched. "How the hell did you even know I was thinking at all?"

"Your gaze roamed up and down my torso, lingering at my waist, and then you squirmed in your seat while you licked your lips. It wasn't hard to discern."

She jerked her gaze down to her root beer and then tugged her hand out of his clasp. "Can we just eat?"

He chuckled. "Yes." He slid two slices of pizza onto a plate and handed it to her before rounding the island and taking a seat on the stool next to hers and serving himself. He sat sideways and spun her just enough to trap one of her knees between both of his. "So, tell me how on earth you were on a date with a man your mom set you up with."

She groaned. "That's where you want to start this conversation?" She didn't really want to talk about her mom. Or Eddie.

"Yep. I already know what you do for a living. You're a flight attendant. I'm sure you have hundreds of work stories, and I'd love to hear all of them, but I want to know about your family first."

She drew in a long breath and met his gaze. "Is this a date? Like a real date?"

He flinched, his eyes narrowing. "Uhhh... I thought so. Does that bother you?"

She licked her lips, trying to figure out how to respond.

"No. It's just unexpected. I didn't know you were going to feed me and ask me personal questions."

He frowned, nodding slowly. "Okay. I get that. It makes sense. Both of our previous encounters have been hot and heavy. And, don't get me wrong, I hope this one ends up that way too. But I thought I should take a step back and get to know you." He reached out and took her chin. "I like you, Libby. It's true you make my cock so hard I can barely concentrate every time I'm around you, but sex isn't the only thing I want from you. I can tell you're a strong woman with a firm head on your shoulders. I thought it might be nice to delve into that brain of yours before I lure you to my bedroom and make you scream my name."

She glanced away, causing him to lose his touch on her chin. She honestly hadn't expected this. It was so...personal. And intimate. Like a date. And apparently it was a date. Not just a fuck.

"Why do I get the feeling you're disappointed?"

She swallowed and lifted her gaze. She needed to be honest with him. "Not disappointed. Just a little stunned. I'm not exactly available for more than the fucking. It's all I have to give you." She cringed when he flinched again.

He stared at her and then slowly chuckled, but he didn't seem angry, just surprised. In fact, he leaned in closer and set a hand on her thigh. "How did we switch roles? Those are usually my lines. I've never had a woman tell me she wanted to skip the dinner part of the evening and move straight to the fucking."

Libby picked up her slice of pizza and took a dramatic bite, finding it to be unexpectedly delicious. "Who said anything about skipping dinner?" she asked. "Damn, this is good." She took another bite.

He laughed and took a large bite of his slice before speaking again. "Talk to me. And please tell me you don't have

53

a boyfriend or something. I assume you don't or you wouldn't have been on a blind date last night."

She shook her head. "No. No boyfriend. What I have is a crazy Guatemalan extended family."

He snickered at that. "We all have crazy families."

She swallowed another bite, took a sip of soda, and then faced him. "Does your mother tell you who you can and can't date?"

His eyes widened. "Shit. Seriously?"

"Yes. It's been drilled into me my entire life. Guatemalans are meant to marry other Guatemalans. No one else is acceptable."

He froze for a moment. "That's… I can't say I've ever met anyone whose parents were quite so rigid. She doesn't like you dating white guys?"

Libby shuddered. "That's putting it mildly. I once dated a Mexican guy and I didn't even tell her. If she thought I was keeping company with a white military man, I think she'd stroke out."

He paused again, his mouth full, before slowly chewing and swallowing. "Okay. Wow. So, I'm the first white guy you've gone out with?"

"Have I gone out with you exactly?" she asked, pointing out her line of thinking. She'd hooked up with him. Once. Run into him at a bar. That didn't count. And here she was, doing what exactly this time? Scratching an itch?

Jason fell into thought while he finished eating, and then he pushed his plate away and faced her again. "This is a date, Libby. The very definition of one. I assume you're attracted to me or you wouldn't have so blatantly flirted with me the night of the rehearsal and then had sex with me the next night."

He was right, but he didn't give her a chance to respond.

He set one hand on the island and the other on the back of her stool, and leaned in closer. "Sex is actually a pretty mild word for what we did and how I felt with you. It was explosive, and you know it. I didn't plan it. It just happened. I've dated vanilla women. Not every woman I meet is interested in my kind of kink. It's not a requirement. But when it works out, it's a bonus."

She didn't move an inch.

He continued. "When I was holding you on the dance floor at the reception, I had a suspicion you were submissive and took a chance. The moment my demand left my lips, I knew I'd been right. You can't deny the chemistry."

She nodded. He was right.

"No woman has ever left me in the middle of the night, however. I was shocked. I thought we'd had an amazing time together. And then you were gone."

She took a breath when he stopped talking, knowing she needed to buck up and be a grownup about this. "I assumed it was a one-night stand. I was trying to avoid the awkward morning dance. The embarrassing part where we can't make eye contact and we both make lame excuses and then part ways."

Jason spun her chair so that she fully faced him. "Did I give you any indication at any point that I wanted you to leave or that I had no intention of seeing you again?"

"No."

"So, really, the one-night stand was more on you than me. You planned it. I went along with it. Don't get me wrong. I wasn't broken up about the idea. Not at first. Who turns down a sexy woman at a wedding? No one. I didn't realize we would have a connection that surpassed the sex any more than you did, but I didn't sneak out in the dead of night."

"It was your room," she half-joked. *How did this evening get off on such a serious note?*

"Libby..."

She sighed. "You're right. I admit it. I went into that

weekend fully hoping to have sex with a buff man in uniform. Sexy military guys have always been my fantasy."

"I'm not sure if I'm flattered or I should spank you."

She flinched and then noticed his slight grin. He was joking. Sort of. Maybe.

"Don't misunderstand," he continued. "I'm so totally going to spank your bottom when we're finished with this conversation. Prepare yourself mentally."

Her body jumped to attention. Those were the words she'd expected the moment she arrived. Not "tell me about your family."

He rolled his eyes. "I would say I've created a monster, but I didn't create you at all. You came to me submissive."

She shook her head. "See, the thing is, I'm not. Submissive I mean. I can't deny you turn me on like no one I've ever met, but I'm not usually like this. I'm strong and independent. I don't take shit from anyone. I don't even ask for help. I've spent my entire life making up for how small I am and the fact that I'm female and Latina. Three strikes against me. But I was born feisty. I rarely ask for help. I figure things out for myself and stand as tall as I can."

His smile was so warm. "I know that, baby girl. You're not an anomaly. Many submissives are actually very strong in their regular lives. It's not unusual at all. But it's a lot of weight to carry around, always being in control of every damn thing, isn't it?"

She shrugged.

"So it's common for people to enjoy a break. Turn over all that power to someone else for a few hours. I realize that night we spent together was probably the first time you'd ever experienced that kind of release. Didn't it feel amazing?"

"Yes," she whispered, barely able to agree with him. This conversation was so deep, bordering on embarrassing. And like everything else, Libby didn't embarrass easily. Or at least she didn't show it or admit it. She met his gaze. "I don't let people boss me around. It's out of my comfort zone."

He lifted a brow. "Except your mom. You let her choose who you date," he pointed out.

She sighed. "Okay. There is that. But I'm really just humoring her. What harm is there in a bunch of blind dates? I've always figured eventually she might get it right. I don't even have to put out any effort."

He chuckled. "Has she gotten it right?"

"No. Never."

"Are all the men she sets you up with as cocky as that Eddie guy from last night?"

"Usually, yes. And I have struggled a bit trying to figure out how you're different. But you are. Your dominance makes me want to…"

"Obey?" he offered, his brows lifted.

She scrunched up her face. "I guess."

He took her hand gently in one of his and rubbed the back of her knuckles with his thumb. "Because my kind of dominance is about bringing you pleasure. I get off on your arousal. It's not all about me."

She nodded. "That's exactly it. That's why I flirted with you. I was kind of desperate to find out what it felt like to have sex with someone more into me. Or maybe I'm just more into you because you're different."

"Are you seeing this Eddie guy again?"

She shook her head. "No. That was a disaster." She shuddered as she remembered him dropping her off last night. He'd wanted to come inside, and she'd feigned exhaustion and managed to put him off. The hardest part about dating random men was then explaining to them later that she didn't want a second date because she just wasn't that into them. Some took it better than others. And, of course, sometimes they weren't into her either. Easy.

"How often does your mom set you up?" His gaze narrowed and he shifted his weight on his stool.

"As often as I let her. It makes her happy. Gives her hope."

"That's pretty fucked-up, Libby." He looked away, grabbing his soda and taking a long drink.

She winced, realizing her situation with her mother sounded far more ridiculous out loud. Obviously, Jason wasn't impressed with her weakness when it came to her mother. *He must think I'm the most pathetic woman alive.* "I know. Pitiful. It keeps the peace. And like I said, perhaps one day she'll find a good one. Somebody I can live with for the long haul." The more she spoke, the more nervous she felt. How had she become such a pushover?

"Live with?" He jerked, his spine straightening. "That's the extent of your life aspirations? Finding a man you can tolerate for fifty years? I feel sorry for that poor bastard."

Libby scrunched up her face and dipped her head. "You sound like Destiny."

"Destiny's a smart woman. You should listen to her. I can't believe you would even entertain the idea of settling for such a low bar." He leaned back, putting some space between them, and ran a hand through his hair. She'd obviously struck a nerve. And she had no one to blame but herself.

On the flip side, Libby also felt defensive. He didn't know her well enough to judge her. "Maybe you're right. Maybe you're not. But I'm not interested in rocking the boat with my mom right now. Dating the men she sets me up with keeps the peace and keeps her off my back. I get tired of listening to her complain about how old I'm getting and how many grandchildren she doesn't have."

Jason stared at her for a moment and then shoved from the island and stood. He gathered up their plates and put them in the dishwasher and then set the box of pizza in the fridge on top of the other box.

She fidgeted nervously while she watched him.

Finally, he turned to face her, setting his hands on the island across from her. "Look, I get that we hardly know each other. We didn't exchange more than a dozen words before tonight. But I'd like to find out where this thing between us might go. I'd like to take you into my room and remind you how damn good we are together. And I can't believe I'm going to say this because such words have never left my lips before, but I'm not hip on sharing you with other guys."

Libby could hardly breathe. Everything about this evening was so unexpected. He had no idea how his oddly possessive words affected her. However, she was in no position to commit to anything serious with him. It had never even occurred to her before. A white guy. Military. The visualization of bringing him to meet her family made her cringe.

Jason rubbed the back of his neck. "Shit. Okay. You need time to process what I've said. I get that. I sprung this on you and you weren't expecting it. Hell, I wasn't either. When I asked you to come over tonight, I pictured laughing over pizza. Flirting. Teasing. And then fucking hard until the sun came up. I didn't mean to let it get all serious. I'm sorry. But it turns out I'm not feeling it."

She flinched. "Not feeling it?" she blurted, interrupting him. Was he suddenly not into her? That made no sense.

He shook his head. "Let me finish. What I mean to say is that I'm into you. It doesn't feel casual to me. My skin was crawling when I saw you with another man."

She swallowed. "Jason, we just met. I'm—"

He held up a hand, stopping her. "I know. I get it. Under normal circumstances, I would wholeheartedly agree. But we have chemistry between us. This is the fourth time I've been in your presence, and it's still there." He set his elbows on the island and leaned in closer.

BECCA JAMESON

She held her breath.

"I want to take you to my bedroom and dominate you until you scream in pleasure. I want to strip off your clothes, spank your bottom, and fuck you so hard you forget everything but how it feels to have me inside you. And I think you want the same thing. I don't think you'd be here if you didn't. You had to put effort into getting my phone number. You made a conscious decision to drive here. You're sitting in my kitchen telling me things I bet you don't often reveal to other people." His voice softened. "You're also squirming on that stool and chewing on your bottom lip. You're free to leave any time. I'm not holding you here against your will. If you want to stay, I'm going to strip your clothes off and rock your world. If you want to leave, I won't hold it against you."

She stared at him wide-eyed. "But you want me to agree to be exclusive with you..."

"Yes. I realize we started this relationship off with intimacy, but it was fucking amazing, and I'm not going to share you. The random blind dates have to stop while you're in my bed."

He had no way of knowing that she didn't sleep around. It wasn't like she would have gone to another man's bed. She never slept with any of her blind dates. She wasn't the sort of woman who slept with *anyone* on the first date anyway.

Except Jason. *Shit. Fuck. Right.* Except Jason... And they hadn't gone on any dates at all when she first slept with him. Did he understand that?

It seemed like she needed to explain better. "I've only slept with three men before you, Jason. None recently. In all three cases, I was in a relationship with them. Exclusive. None of them lasted long, probably because the sex was bad." She added that last part on a murmur.

"The sex with me will never be bad, baby girl." The

60

promise in his tone made her shudder. God, she loved it when he spoke to her like that.

This entire evening had been about her. She knew nothing about his family or why he'd left the military recently or what he did for a living. She feared the more she learned about him the more she would like him. That hadn't really been in the cards. At least that's what she'd told herself. Maybe she'd secretly hoped for more, but she hadn't had any way to picture anything beyond amazing sex so far.

"So, you want to see what my bedroom looks like? Or would you rather end the evening right now?"

There was no turning him down. Not a chance. He made her heart beat fast, her clit throb, and her pussy weep. She didn't have the foggiest idea how she would get out of her mother's constant setups, but she would figure something out.

"I'd like to see your bedroom, please."

He smiled as he rounded the island and came to her. He spun her stool around so they were face to face, and then he cupped her cheeks in his palms and lowered his mouth. The moment their lips touched, she melted. He was a damn good kisser. Assertive without being pushy. Confident in a way he had earned. She let him guide her, responding to every lick and suck with her own exploration.

She flattened her palms on his rock-hard chest, melting against him. No one had ever kissed her like this before. Even that one simple thing was different with him. She was on fire, wishing he wouldn't bother with the bedroom and strip her right here in the kitchen.

When he broke the kiss, she was breathless and aroused.

He slid his hands down to her shoulders and then lower to span her waist. His palms were so large his thumbs grazed the undersides of her breasts as he spoke again. "I know you work weird hours and days, but I want to see you in between."

"I'd like that." She really would. As stressful as this night had been so far, she wanted to see him every chance possible.

"Send me your schedule."

"Okay."

He stepped closer, nudging her knees apart. "When you're here in my home, you're mine."

And that did it. Her pussy wept, her arousal soaking the inside of her jeans. Her breasts ached. She had a sudden urge to squeeze them. The intense look on his face alone pushed her over the edge.

"Yes, Sir." *Holy. Shit.* Those words slipped out without her consideration. They just happened.

Jason looked beyond pleased. "That's my girl. Now, while I finish cleaning up the kitchen, you go find my room. Take everything off. I want you on your hands and knees on the edge of my bed, sideways, your sweet bottom offered up for my palm."

"Yes, Sir." The words were far breathier that second time but spoken with confidence all the same. She slid off the stool and made her way toward the opening to the hallway she'd seen on the other side of the living room.

She was filled with a combination of fear and longing. She was really going to do this. Submit to this powerful man. A man she was falling for. She needed to keep her head on straight and guard her heart. Surely this couldn't be more than a fling. A way to get him out of her system. She wasn't sure how long that might take, but she needed to remind herself often. Nothing else was believable. She'd heard of people meeting and instantly falling hard enough for each other to bang every chance they got. She was also realistic enough to know it wasn't sustainable. She wouldn't dare hope for something like that.

For now, all that mattered was finding his room and letting go of her control. She didn't need to question the sex.

It would be phenomenal. She shivered when she remembered he intended to spank her. But she'd suspected that from his text. She'd been curious ever since. Her nipples were swollen and needy, abrading against the lace of her bra.

With a deep breath, she entered his room and soaked in his surroundings. The kitchen and living room had told her nothing about him. This room, however, was finished. It had a strong masculine feel. The huge bed was the focal point, high off the ground with four posts. She shuddered, imagining what kinds of things he might do with those posts.

After a quick perusal of his mahogany furniture, his navy bedding, and the gorgeous hardwood floors, she quickly removed all her clothes and hoisted herself up onto his bed, getting into the position he'd requested.

She was really doing this. Decisively. This wasn't like their "one-night stand." She was now consciously and intentionally submitting to the only man who'd ever made her heart beat as fast as it was right now.

CHAPTER 8

Jason took his time cleaning the kitchen. There wasn't really anything else to do. He was stalling to give Libby a few moments alone. He knew she was rattled. She would need to gather her thoughts and have some time to undress.

He also knew she would follow his orders.

This evening had not gone quite as he'd expected. Not even close. He had fully intended to spend time getting to know her on a more personal level because he did honestly like her, but he hadn't expected to demand exclusivity. That had snuck up on him. It was crazy enough that he wanted Libby to spend the night in his bed. He had no idea where his possessive instinct came from. He was heading into dangerous territory. The last woman he trusted with his heart stomped on it and made a fool out of him. He swore he would never let something like that happen to him again. He would not.

Were there red flags flying? Yes. But he wasn't as naïve as he'd been three years ago. He was also smarter and more hardened. He just needed to be careful. Keep his eyes open.

Libby is not Veronica, he reminded himself, shaking the unwelcome thoughts from his mind.

He was still reeling at the idea that Libby's parents, her mom in particular, seemed to have as much control over her as they did. She was twenty-eight years old. A grown woman. Educated. Intelligent. Outspoken. Strong. The whole package. How was she still under her mother's thumb?

Part of him was taken aback by the fact that she hadn't seen him as more than a hot fuck. *How ironic. I finally meet a woman who makes me look twice, and she pulls a one-eighty on me and wants nothing but sex?*

He smiled as he wiped off the counter. *Serves me right. How many times have I been in the opposite situation?*

Truth be told, although he hadn't contacted her for the last six months since their night together, she'd been on his mind. She'd featured in many of his dreams. He'd begun to think he'd exaggerated their night together, blown it out of proportion. And then he'd seen her last night, and instantly he'd been reminded that what he'd experienced had been real.

He'd actually been a little bitter that she'd left without a word that morning. Irrationally, since he'd been known to do the same thing on occasion, and who the hell was he that the tables couldn't be turned on him? It humbled him.

He understood. It made sense that she would assume their night had been a one-off. He'd thought the same thing at first, too. It was easier for her to sneak out and avoid the awkward morning after. He got that. It was the reason he hadn't called her.

But now. *Jesus.* He ran a hand through his hair and closed his eyes, trying to rein in his reactions to her. There was no doubt he understood her better, and nothing she'd said had made him back off. In fact, if anything, he viewed her as even more of a challenge.

Your mother doesn't let you date white guys?

He smirked in his mind. *We'll just see about that.*

He couldn't believe he'd given her an ultimatum, halfway through their first real date. Their one-night stand couldn't count because they hadn't exchanged enough words to know anything about each other. What they had learned, however, was far more important in his book. They had chemistry like no one he'd ever been with.

Nevertheless, he was surprised by his insistence that she not date anyone else. The words had flown out of his mouth before he could stop them. On top of that, he had no regrets. He probably shouldn't feel this possessive, but he did. He didn't own the woman after one night of fucking and a half-date.

Except he did. At least for now. He *did* own her.

And he was about to show her what it meant to be owned by him.

After a last quick glance around the kitchen, he took a deep breath and padded toward his bedroom.

The moment he rounded the corner, his breath hitched. She was exactly where he'd told her to be, on her hands and knees on the edge of the bed, her fantastic ass waiting for his palm.

She was also shivering. *Not surprising.*

He stepped up behind her, set his palms on her sexy bottom and molded his fingers to her skin, squeezing and releasing so she would relax. "Has anyone ever spanked you before?"

"No," she whispered. Her glorious hair hung down to shield her face. He considered gathering it back and putting a band on it but then decided to give her that curtain for now. A small sense of privacy that might help calm her nerves.

"I can smell your arousal, little one."

Her sweet little body shuddered and she inched her knees together.

He tapped her thighs. "Spread open for me."

Her breath hitched delightfully as she obeyed him.

"Farther, baby girl. Knees wide. I want you to feel the vulnerability." He continued to rub her smooth skin as she did his bidding. "Good girl. I bet you're soaking wet."

She whimpered.

God, she was precious. Every inch of her. He'd been with plenty of women over the years and none had grabbed him so thoroughly by the balls as Libby. He wanted to shrug out of his jeans and fuck her sweet little pussy right now.

Instead, he would spank her until she fully understood what it meant to feel his palm on her bottom, and then he would make her come so hard she screamed. Only then would he slide his cock into her heat. It would be worth the wait.

Jason smoothed his palms down the backs of her thighs, intentionally pulling her labia apart with his thumbs. He couldn't resist the urge to touch her pussy, so he reached between her legs and dragged two fingers through her folds. Soaked. As expected. "My little girl is so needy."

Another whimper as she pushed her bottom out toward him, silently asking for more.

He took his hand away. "Not yet, little one. You'll experience your first spanking without reaching orgasm. It will be hard, but I want you to control yourself. I'll let you come when I'm finished."

She turned her face in his direction, shaking her hair out of the way to see him. Her confused expression spoke volumes.

He chuckled and cupped her face gently. "Oh yeah, trust me. You're going to love the feel of my palm on your bottom. It's so erotic. Take a few breaths and try not to stiffen." He released her cheek, angled to one side of her, and set his palm on the small of her back to steady her and ground her.

When he lifted his hand to give her the first taste of what it meant to be spanked, his cock grew thicker against his jeans. A second later, he landed the first swat, keeping it light. She lifted her head, her chest dipping as she rocked forward slightly.

He didn't give her a chance to think. The second swat landed slightly lower, a bit harder, letting his pinky hit her thigh.

Her belly and chest dipped lower as she elongated her neck and moaned. *Beautiful. Just as he'd expected.*

He picked up the pace, spanking her all over, heating her smooth skin. Her bottom was gorgeous as her dark skin darkened further. After a few more swats, he lowered his aim, knowing if he struck at the juncture of her bottom and thighs, it would vibrate to her pussy.

Her body stiffened, unintelligible sounds coming from her mouth. Before she had a chance to process what she was feeling, he slid his hand between her legs and thrust his thumb into her wet heat. He immediately found her clit with his fingers and rubbed it.

She rocked back again, moaning louder. "Jason," she cried out. "Oh, God."

He held her as still as he could with his hand on her lower back, but it was fucking sexy the way she writhed, rutting back and forth, trying to get more purchase. He knew what she needed; she needed to have her sweet pussy filled with his cock. And she would get that. After she gave him the first orgasm.

"That's it, little one. Ride my hand. Let it go. Come for me."

It took only moments for her to shatter around his thumb and fingers, her body trembling as she moaned through the pulses of her orgasm.

He watched her closely. The moment she winced from the sensitivity, he removed his fingers and guided her onto her side.

She was breathing heavily, not even bothering to swipe her hair from her face as he watched her. No one had ever been so preciously sexy to him. Every new thing he did with her brought that knowledge closer to home.

Libby was pure, raw. Not an ounce of deceit. She was nothing like Veronica. When things ended with Veronica, he'd been able to look back and see the signs. She had used him. Nothing about her intentions had ever been this genuine. Not in retrospect. She might have enjoyed their sex, but she'd exaggerated her reaction to everything as if it were some kind of game to her.

Jason shook the past from his head and smiled as he rolled Libby to her back next, brushed the hair from her face, and lifted her arms over her head. She was so pliant. Sated. *Gorgeous.* He bent her knees and spread them open next, pressing them with authority into the bed.

She blinked up at him, her eyes glazed, a soft smile on her lips.

Oh yeah, I'm in so much trouble with this one.

Her hair was spread out around her, the thick mass of it gorgeously tussled. He loved the tone of her skin, and he took a moment to drag a finger up her thigh and across her belly, circling a nipple before tapping it lightly.

She sighed, and for a moment he thought she might fall asleep on him, but then she arched her chest into his touch. "Jason... Please..."

"Please what, baby girl?"

"I need you."

He chuckled, his cock extremely pleased. "Is that so? You're not too wrung out from having your sweet little bottom spanked and then fucking yourself on my fingers?"

She blinked a few times and then smiled at him before glancing away. "You spanked me."

"I did." He stopped tormenting her nipple to unbutton his

jeans and shrug out of them. After grabbing a condom from his nightstand, he set his hands on her waist and smoothed them up to cup her breasts, flicking his thumbs over her nipples.

She moaned again.

"Does it embarrass you that I spanked you?"

"Yes. I mean, not at the time. But now I feel kinda weird about it."

"So..." He scooted her back on the bed and climbed over her, dropping to his elbows beside her head to hover over her body. "What you're saying is that you weren't too embarrassed to be spanked, but you're embarrassed that you liked it."

She bit her lip and met his gaze.

He kissed her nose. "It's perfectly normal, baby girl. No reason to feel weird about it. You like being dominated. I like dominating you. It's a win-win." He reached between her legs and found her still dripping.

She lifted her hips into his touch, so eager, a whimper escaping her lips again.

"You want my cock, little one?"

"Yes, Sir. Please."

God, he loved it when she called him Sir. He would never insist upon it. He preferred it come naturally. But it made his dick jump. He rose onto his hands and then lifted one to tap her sweet body. "Roll onto your belly again, baby." When she complied, he slid his knees between hers and then rose up to lift her hips. "On your knees again."

Libby slid toward him, letting him situate her where he wanted her.

"Lower to your elbows, little one. You can relax your arms."

She practically purred as she followed his instructions, her body trembling in the way he now knew it did when she had a rush of arousal. He'd seen the signs several times now. She settled on her elbows, her face turned to one side, resting on her cheek. She even clasped her hands above her head.

Jason gently brushed her hair away from her face and stroked a finger down her cheek. "Good girl."

Another shudder. She liked it when he praised her. She followed the shudder with a soft, pliant sigh.

He palmed her bottom, still warm from his spanking. Her skin was darker from his swats, too. *Sexy as hell.* He hadn't struck her very hard this first time, but now that he was certain she'd enjoyed it, he would up his game next time.

There would be a next time. There had to be.

He nudged her knees wider with his, opening her sex. Deciding not to touch her where she most craved it just yet, he grabbed the condom from the bed, ripped it open, and rolled it down his length. He needed to be inside her.

Holding her hip with one hand, he lined himself up with her entrance and thrust into her all the way to the hilt.

She cried out unintelligibly, her hands fisting the comforter now while she pressed her bottom back toward him.

He gritted his teeth, knowing that like the last time he'd been inside her six months ago, he was not going to last long. He held her hips tight, keeping her from squirming while he focused on anything but how damn good it felt to have her pussy wrapped around his cock. Failing that, he blew out a breath and let himself ease out of her warmth before thrusting back into her again.

Libby continued to shove herself closer to him, pushing with her hands as if somehow she could get more contact.

He lifted one hand and swatted her reddened bottom. "Stay still, baby girl."

She moaned. "Please. Oh God, Jason. I'm so close again already. I need…"

"I know you are, little one. But you need to stop squirming. I'll decide when and if you come. Understood?"

Another delicious shiver all down her body. "Yes, Sir." She stopped trying to control him, though he could tell by the tight grip she had on the comforter it wasn't easy.

He watched as he slid in and out of her, the sight almost his undoing by itself. She felt so damn good wrapped around him. The only chance he had of ever lasting longer than a few minutes inside her would be if he took her more than once in the same night.

He kept his movements as slow as he could manage, but every inch of friction pushed him closer to nirvana no matter what speed he assumed.

Needing to hear her cry out again, he reached around her belly and found her clit. The moment he stroked the swollen nub, she lifted her face. "Jason..." Her voice was strained.

"It's okay, little one. Come with me. Do it now, baby."

She clenched her pussy at his command, her body pulsing around his cock, a long moan coming from her lips.

He thrust harder as he pressed against her clit, holding his breath as he reached his peak. He had never enjoyed a woman as much as he did this one, and that thought didn't escape him as his orgasm pulsed deep inside her.

He was totally wrapped around her finger, and it would be impossible for her not to find that out.

Jason lowered her to her side finally, easing out of her. He wished he could stay inside her warmth forever, but that wasn't practical. Instead, he patted her ruddy ass and slid off the bed.

After a quick trip to the bathroom to dispose of the condom and clean himself up, he returned to her side, rolled her sleepy body onto her back, and spread her legs so he could wipe her pussy.

She moaned, her eyes closed, her body pliant.

He hauled her up the bed, settled a pillow under her head, and then grinned to himself as he had an idea.

She didn't move a muscle while he reached into the drawer next to his bed and pulled out the perfect toy. She didn't fight him as he lifted her left arm over her head either. It wasn't until the click of the handcuff disturbed the silence in the room that she opened her eyes.

"What are you doing?" she murmured.

He attached the other end of the handcuff to the bedpost. There were two feet of chain between the cuffs, giving her plenty of wiggle room. "Making sure you can't sneak out on me in the middle of the night again."

Her eyes widened, and her mouth fell open. "You can't be serious."

"Very." He wiggled his brows. "I'm exhausted. I'll sleep much better knowing you can't escape." He climbed over her, pulled the covers up both their bodies, and maneuvered her onto her side so he could spoon her sweet body from behind.

"Jason." Her voice was high-pitched.

He slid his hand up between her breasts and held her close. "Sleep, little one." He couldn't keep from smiling at her shock but tried to keep his mirth out of his voice.

"You expect me to sleep handcuffed to your bed?"

"Yep."

She tugged on his hand with her free one. "I promise I won't sneak out."

"Mmm." He flipped his palm over and grabbed her smaller hand with his, wrapping his fingers around her fist. When she squirmed, he rolled her onto her belly and slid his palm down to her warm bottom. He gave a squeeze and then a quick, hard swat.

She gasped, but a moan followed. "Jason…" Her voice was breathy.

"Stop fighting me, Libby."

"But—"

Another swat, and this time he reached between her legs and stroked his fingers through her folds, proving what he already knew. She was wet.

Her whimper was musical, and she ground her pussy against his fingers.

He withdrew his hand, trailing her wetness up over her bottom with his fingers until she shivered. "You'll follow my rules in this bed, little one, and right now, the rule is that you'll sleep cuffed to the bedpost. If you continue arguing, I'll spank you again, but this time, I won't let you come." He flattened his hand on her lower back.

She squirmed under his palm.

He slid his hand down to her bottom again and squeezed her cheeks. "You want more?"

She shook her head. "No, Sir."

Those words made his cock stiff, but he ignored it. "Good girl." He rolled her back to her side and snuggled up behind her fucking sexy little body, clasping her free hand in his once again between her breasts. His lips found her neck. "Sleep now."

She sighed. "Yes, Sir."

It took her a long time to relax and settle down. Until then, he remained wide awake, loving every little noise she made and the way she wiggled in his arms. Nothing helped his dick stand down, but he enjoyed every second.

Eventually, she fell asleep, and he followed right behind her.

CHAPTER 9

Libby woke up smiling. She was on her side, snuggled deep under the covers. What woke her was the hand sliding up her thigh and over her hip. The hand was attached to the warm body at her back. *Jason...*

His fingers continued their slow glide along her side until they slid around to cup her breast. She hadn't moved yet, not until he flicked his thumb over her nipple, making her moan and arch her chest into his palm.

He chuckled behind her. "You like that, huh?"

"Mmm."

He used his knee to nudge her top thigh forward, bending her leg, opening her pussy. "I can smell your arousal, little one," he whispered as he set his lips on her neck, just behind her ear.

She moaned again, fully alert. Needy. She fisted the sheets in her hand as she braced herself. She'd never spent the night with a man. Never awakened in someone's arms. Never had mind-blowing sex only to be aroused all over again a few hours later.

Damn, it felt good. Butterflies jumped around in her belly as he pinched her nipple lightly.

She started to roll toward him but came up short when she tugged on her left arm and was reminded she was cuffed to the bed.

Jason slid his hand up her arm to her wrist and pressed it against the mattress. "Leave your hand here, baby." He proceeded to kiss her neck, nuzzling her and nipping at her skin until she squirmed. "You're so wiggly," he mused as he rolled her to her back and lifted her right hand toward the opposite corner of the bed.

She met his gaze for the first time this morning, blinking in the dim light coming in through the blinds. The look in his eyes was predatory, and it made her body quiver. "I need to fuck you. You've had me hard all night. Are you too sore?"

Her face heated at the intimacy as he stared at her, making her feel even more naked than simply not having any clothes on. It felt like he was looking into her soul. "No." The word was breathy.

He rolled away from her, still holding her wrist in place, the blankets and sheets went with him, the soft material dragging over her nipples until they stiffened.

She heard the drawer opening on the bedside table and wondered what else he had in there. When she heard the clinking noise of a chain, she twisted her face to see a second set of handcuffs just as he secured her wrist. *How many of those does he have?*

She drew her knees together as she considered the possibility that he might have two more sets. The thought of being secured spread-eagled on his bed both frightened and excited her.

After clasping the second cuff to the bedpost, Jason returned to her side, leaning on his hip as he met her gaze again. He flattened his palm on her belly, teasing her skin with his fingers. His palm was so large that it spanned her entire stomach.

"Jason," she whimpered. Her nipples were stiff points, and wetness had pooled between her legs. She'd never been restrained like this. It was heady while at the same time unnerving.

His gaze roamed down her frame. His voice was low and calm. "Let me look at you. We were in a frenzy last night. I didn't get a chance to stare at your sexy little body. It's been six months. Let me look."

She shivered under his gaze.

He slid his hand up to cup one of her breasts, so lightly, thumbing her nipple until she moaned and arched her chest.

"I love the way you respond to me."

She loved it too, even though it scared her at the same time. Libby was always in control. Of everything. Nothing happened in her life that she didn't plan and dictate. Not until Jason came along. He controlled everything, bringing her body to life in a way she hadn't known was possible.

He cupped her other breast next, teasing it in the same way. "Open your legs for me, little one."

She realized she was gripping her knees together, keeping the intense arousal at bay as much as possible. At his command, she drew her knees up, squeezing them tighter.

A sudden tight pinch to her nipple made her gasp.

"Legs, baby. Spread them open."

She dropped her feet to the mattress and let her knees fall apart. *What am I hiding from him, anyway?*

Jason released her breast to crawl between her legs. He grabbed her knees, pushed them higher and wider, and then slid his hands down her inner thighs. His fingers grazed the edges of her pussy, not touching her anywhere she most craved.

She rolled her head to one side and bit into her lower lip,

77

fighting against the embarrassment of being so thoroughly inspected.

"I love the way you shaved for me, little one. Did you do this yesterday?"

The question was so personal. "Yes," she breathed. She certainly hadn't shaved for Eddie. She'd had no intention of sleeping with Eddie. But she'd known with certainty she would be sleeping with Jason. Just as she had the last time she'd been with him.

He parted her labia, and the moment the air in the room hit her open sex, she quivered. He released her legs and moved one palm up to her belly, using his thumb to pull the hood back from her clit. With his other hand, he spread her lower lips apart again and dragged his fingers through her wetness.

She nearly shot off the bed when he flicked her clit.

"Keep your legs open for me, or I'll cuff them like I did your wrists."

Her mouth fell open.

"You have the sexiest body I've ever seen, Libby. I love how it responds to me. I'm going to eat your sweet pussy now until you scream, and then I'm going to fuck you until you scream louder."

The play-by-play he tended to give her made her hornier.

Libby sucked in a breath when he lowered himself between her legs, gripped her thighs, and reverently kissed her sex before dragging his tongue through her wetness and then suckling her clit.

She moaned, her heels digging into the mattress. In seconds, she was close to coming. Did she have permission to come? Would he spank her if she didn't wait for his instructions? "Sir…"

He nipped her clit with his teeth and lifted his gaze. "You need to come already, baby?"

"Yes. Please." Her knees quivered.

He didn't say anything before he dipped his head down and thrust his tongue into her. His hands slid under her ass and gripped her cheeks as he lifted her pussy toward his face.

When his lips wrapped around her clit, she couldn't stop the waves of pleasure from consuming her. She would just have to endure the punishment if it came. Right now, all she cared about was the incredible release. Her body shook with spasms as she moaned loudly.

Jason slowly eased off, licking and kissing her as he gradually withdrew his attention. He wiped his mouth on the sheets and then stretched across her to grab something else from the bedside table.

When he came back between her legs, she was still panting, and her channel clenched with the need to be filled. He ripped the condom open with his teeth and then rolled it down his length while she watched. "You're gorgeous when you come, Libby."

She swallowed.

He dropped onto his palms, hovering over her. After searching her face, he smiled. "You need my cock more than your next breath, don't you?"

"Yes, Sir," she murmured.

Finally, he lined up with her deprived entrance and thrust home.

Her breath caught in her lungs at the stretch. Even though they'd had sex last night, it was still an incredibly tight fit. He was huge. He dropped over her, holding some of his weight off her by his elbows, and cupped her face. His mouth descended, and the moment he kissed her, he started thrusting. Hard. Deep. *So good.*

The taste of her own arousal on his mouth was exhilarating. She kissed him back with as much passion as he did her, tongues dueling for control, lips frantic, teeth bumping into teeth.

She couldn't get a full breath, and she didn't care. Every ounce of her concentration was on the way he filled her over and over. The friction. The pressure. The building need.

She wrapped her legs around his thighs and lifted and lowered her butt with every thrust. He ground the base of his cock against her clit, making her moan into his mouth.

Suddenly, he broke the kiss, drew back an inch, and watched her face as he continued fucking her. Nothing had ever felt this good. Every time they had sex was better than the last. The addition of the handcuffs made her feel controlled in a way she'd never imagined enjoying in real life.

While she was in his bed, she didn't have to think or make decisions or prove herself to anyone. All she had to do was obey his demands and enjoy the ride. *And boy, can he take me for a ride.*

He picked up the pace, his jaw tightening. "Come, baby girl. I want to feel your pussy contracting around my cock before my release."

If anyone would have suggested there would ever come a day when she could come with a man let alone on command, she would have laughed them out the door. But her body responded to Jason's demands every time. Her pussy gripped him harder, and the next time he ground down on her clit, she shattered. Her vision swam and her hearing dulled as though she were underwater.

But she didn't miss the fact that he got what he wanted. She screamed. Loudly. Her release all-consuming.

Waves of pleasure consumed her as she pulsed around him over and over, loving every moment of her release.

Jason was still pulsing into her as she regained some sense of time and place.

She was addicted to this man, and that was a dangerous

place to be. *How the hell am I ever going to explain this to my parents?*

She wasn't. It was out of the question. She was going to keep this man to herself and see what happened. She would just have to put her mother off every time she suggested another blind date. Jason had made himself perfectly clear—he wasn't sharing her. And she couldn't blame him. The thought of sitting across the table from one random man after the other didn't appeal to her at all. Besides, she intended to spend every moment of free time with Jason, not her mother's blind date choices.

How long could she play this game? What if this arrangement didn't burn itself out? It couldn't go on forever. It wasn't as if she could bring Jason home to meet her parents. Ever. But what if this didn't fizzle out? What if she grew more and more attached to him?

So she told herself it was a fling. She was scratching an itch. Fucking hot sex she wasn't about to turn down. She had no clear picture of the future, but no way would she run from this arrangement right now, because the thought of doing that made her shudder.

She trembled as Jason dropped onto her body, barely supporting his weight off her. He was breathing heavily. She had no idea what the hell the future might bring, but for now, she fully intended to seize the day.

CHAPTER 10

"You're spoiling me," Libby stated as she accepted the plate of food Jason slid across the island toward her.

He chuckled as he grabbed a second plate and rounded the island to sit next to her. "It's just breakfast. If you hadn't snuck out on me the first time you slept in my bed, I would have taken you out to eat."

She rolled her eyes. "How long are you going to continue mentioning that little detail," she asked as she picked up her fork and took a bite of pancakes.

He swallowed his bite and then winked at her. "Probably forever."

She picked up a strip of bacon and savored the crispy bite before speaking again. "I've never been in a relationship with a Dominant before, so pardon my ignorance, but I'm surprised you didn't order me to make breakfast for you." She lifted her gaze to meet his.

He smiled and then set a hand on her lower back and smoothed it up under her hair to her neck. The only thing she wore was one of his T-shirts, which he'd handed her after he finished washing her in the shower and then drying her off. Her clothes had been nowhere in sight.

She'd thought it wise not to say a word. After all, his T-shirt reached nearly to her knees. It wasn't as though she was naked.

Jason kissed her forehead before responding. "You're not a domestic submissive, baby. Our D/s relationship is strictly in the bedroom. It's sexual."

She nodded. *Interesting.*

"If you want to cook for me someday, be my guest, but I'll never require it. Nor will I require you to clean or kneel at my feet. I'm not that kind of Dom. My interest is in making you scream when you come." He winked.

She shifted her weight on her stool, squeezing her thighs together. The mention of making her come had her hot and bothered all over again. And the picture he painted was so damn inviting. Who would turn him down?

"Tell me what your schedule looks like," he inquired. "When do I get you back in my bed?"

"I work this evening and then about twelve hours Monday and Tuesday. I'm off Wednesday."

"Do you usually spend the night out of town?"

"Sometimes. Monday night I'll be in Vegas."

He lifted his brows. "That's cool."

She shrugged. "Not really. I'll be exhausted. I'll only have about nine hours off. And I don't gamble." It was time to turn the tables. "I know nothing about you. Tell me why you left the military and what you're doing in Dallas."

He waited until he swallowed and took a sip of coffee. "Honestly, I was exhausted. I did three tours, and it was time to get out. Plus, I had a job offer from a buddy of mine here in Dallas that I couldn't refuse."

"What job is that?" she asked as she took another bite of pancake.

"My friend Jake owns a computer programming business called Westside Programmers. Freelance. It's what I'm trained in. I did programming for the Army. He opened the business a few years ago. Kraft introduced us a while back. He also works for Jake now. When I got out, Jake offered me a job. I took it. I love the flexibility. Most days I work from home. Some days I go to a client's office and deal with their issues on-site."

"That's cool. I know nothing about computers. I can check my email and manage my social media, and that's about it."

"I enjoy the challenge. Every day is different." He leaned in closer. "See? There's a benefit to dating me. If you ever need computer help…"

"Good point." She giggled. "Your friend, his name is Kraft?"

"Yep. I mean that's his nickname from when we served. Even before that, really. The man eats boxed mac and cheese like it's going out of style. I think it's gross. We all gave him shit until we started calling him Kraft. His real name is Mack Carter."

"And they call you Hatch. What's the story behind that?"

He finished his pancakes and pushed the plate away. "It's not a nickname I would have chosen. I can tell you that." He sighed. "We were in Iraq and I was unloading an armored vehicle. I forgot to secure the driver's hatch. When I bumped into it, it fell against my head. Thank God I was wearing my Kevlar helmet or I wouldn't have been so lucky. As it was, I ended up with a broken nose, eight stitches in my brow, and a permanent nickname."

She gasped. "You could have been killed. Thank God you were okay."

He set a hand on her thigh and rubbed. "Yep. And all my brain cells are still functioning too, which is why I'm going to set these dishes in the sink while you head back to the bedroom and take this shirt off. I've decided the visual of you kneeling at my feet is appealing. I'd like to watch you wrap your mouth around my cock while you do it though."

She licked her lips. The idea appealed to her a lot. After all, he'd had his mouth on her pussy several times. So far, she hadn't returned the favor. She had a few hours left before she needed to get back to her apartment and get ready for work. She couldn't think of a better way to spend her time than another round in his bedroom.

CHAPTER 11

It was Wednesday morning before Libby got a text from Jason. Granted, she'd told him she had to work nearly nonstop until then, but she'd found herself checking her phone every chance she got for those two days. Except for the single rose she's received on Monday morning, she'd had no contact with him. It was sweet of him to think of her though. It brightened her day.

Meanwhile, her mother had called four times and left messages to ask how her date with Eddie had gone and when she was planning to see him again. Libby's saving grace was the fact that she could let her mother's calls go to voicemail pretty often and then blame her inattentiveness on her flight schedule.

Libby was still in bed, but she snatched up her phone from the nightstand the moment the text came through.

Hey, baby girl. I assume you made it home okay last night. I was thinking about you.

She breathed a sigh of relief. He didn't need to know how anxious she'd been to hear from him.

I did. Thank you for asking. I got home after midnight. I'm still lying in bed.

I like the visual. Can I interest you in a real date tonight? One that involves dinner at a restaurant?

She smiled broadly as she texted him back.

Sounds great.

Good. Text me your address. I'll pick you up at seven. No panties.

She nearly dropped the phone on her chest when she read those last two words. Her body responded too, shooting from zero to ten on the arousal scale in seconds.

Libby had never considered herself a sex fiend. Not until she'd met Jason anyway. Starting six months ago, she'd found herself masturbating with far more frequency. It became second nature for her to close her eyes and slide into an imaginary world where Jason hovered over her, dominating her so deliciously that she'd been able to come within minutes every time.

Since their date Saturday night that led into half of Sunday, she'd had even more material to work with.

Now, she dropped the phone at her side and wiggled out of her panties. What better way to start the day than to obey his command immediately while also taking care of her pulsing desire?

Seconds after swirling her fingers around her clit, her phone pinged again. She considered ignoring it but didn't want to miss another text from Jason, so she reluctantly stopped touching herself to reach for the phone.

Before she had a chance to see the text, it rang in her hand. Incoming call from Jason. She flushed, feeling as though he'd caught her masturbating when he couldn't possibly know that. Her fingers were shaking as she answered. "Hey." Her voice was too deep. She cleared her throat.

"Hey, yourself," he responded, chuckling. "Busy?"

"Uh... No?"

"Is that a question?"

"No. I mean I'm not busy. I'm not even up yet."

"You mentioned that, and then you didn't respond to my last text, so I thought maybe you'd decided to masturbate."

She sucked in a breath, shocked by his bluntness. *What the hell am I supposed to say in response?*

"I was right, wasn't I?"

She cringed. *How the hell was I caught touching myself by someone who isn't in the house?* "Maybe?"

He laughed. "Maybe? Are you wearing panties?"

"No. I was. But no. Now I'm not."

"Were your fingers touching your pussy when I called?"

She swallowed. "Yes."

"That's kind of the definition of masturbating, little one."

Her face heated as she bit into her lip. The phone vibrated a second later, indicating Jason wanted to switch to FaceTime. She nearly died as she accepted the new connection. Her hands were shaking as she held the phone up.

"Hey," he said softly, smirking.

"Hey," she repeated yet again.

"Your cheeks are red."

"Are they?" She licked her lips. Her body was trembling for reasons she couldn't understand.

"Definitely. Lift your knees, spread them wide, and prop

the phone against your thigh so I can watch your face while you masturbate."

She stopped breathing. "Uh…"

"Do it, baby. You wanted to come. I want to watch."

She slowly lifted her knees, leaving the covers over her so that they pulled tight between her thighs. It was easy to set the phone down between her legs, leaning it against the blanket. It was angled just right to include her face. She was breathing heavily. "Not sure I can do this, Jason."

He smiled. "I know you can. Forget I'm watching. You can even close your eyes if you want. Fuck your pretty little pussy for me. Were you going to use your fingers or a vibrator?"

"Uh…" She couldn't believe they were having this conversation. "I hadn't gotten that far yet. I would have grabbed a vibrator eventually," she confessed.

"Good point. It had only been thirty seconds. Just long enough for you to yank off your panties and run your fingers through your folds."

God, he's good. "Yes." *Is he psychic?*

"Do you always wear panties?"

"Yes." The only times she'd gone without had been Friday night when she'd given them to him outside the bar and Saturday night when she'd gone to his house without them under her jeans. She even slept in panties…except the two nights she'd slept with him.

His voice dropped and she thought he leaned forward. "Can you make yourself come with your fingers alone?"

"Not likely." But as horny as she was, maybe she was wrong. Maybe she *could* come from finger stimulation.

"Let's try. Touch yourself, baby girl. Stroke your fingers through your pussy."

She was trembling as she followed his directions, and moaned the moment her fingers dragged through her folds.

"Are you wet, little one?"

"Yes, Sir."

"Good. Use that to play with your clit. Don't be gentle. I don't want you to drag this out. I want you to come hard and fast. Flick your clit rapidly and then pinch it."

She closed her eyes and did as he instructed, not wanting to watch him watching her.

"That's a good girl. Move faster. Thrust three fingers from your other hand into your cunt while you continue tormenting your clit."

She obeyed him again, unable to do otherwise. She sucked in a breath at the stretch from her fingers buried deep inside her. Her other hand worked furiously as her clit throbbed and swelled.

"Thrust your fingers, baby girl. Don't worry about the phone. I can hear you if it falls."

She stiffened her legs as she plunged her fingers in and out of her sopping wet channel. She was painfully close already. She sucked in a breath and held it, trying to keep from coming so fast.

"Don't hold back, Libby," he demanded. "Come for me. Do it now."

As if her pussy followed orders only from him, she came, the rush of her orgasm slamming to the surface so fast she gasped. It wasn't enough. It left her panting with need.

"God, you're gorgeous. Do you feel better?"

"Not really, Sir," she admitted.

He smirked. "I bet your pussy is pulsing with the need for my cock."

"Yes," she breathed. Her legs were shaking as she met his gaze on the screen.

"Good. I didn't want that orgasm to be very satisfying, you naughty girl. Now, stop touching yourself. Keep your greedy fingers away from your pussy for the rest of the day. If you're a good girl later, maybe I'll let you come again tonight."

She swallowed, embarrassed and intrigued and excited and nervous.

"I gotta get back to work. Find something to keep yourself busy, little one. Spend the day in a T-shirt and no panties, but keep your hands above your waist. Understood?"

"Yes, Sir," she whispered, already shuddering at the thought.

"Wear a skirt or a dress tonight. No panties."

"Yes, Sir."

He smiled. "See you at seven." And then he ended the call.

She was left staring at the screen, wondering how the hell he'd just hijacked not only her orgasm but her entire day. If she spent the day in nothing but a T-shirt, she wouldn't be able to get him out of her mind.

But he knew that.

He was a devious Dom.

CHAPTER 12

Jason had a hell of a time concentrating the entire day. He'd been shocked by how easily he'd guessed that Libby was masturbating and then how quickly he'd managed to control her orgasm over the phone. *Sexy as fuck.*

His dick had been hard all day too, and he'd denied it just as he'd denied her. He couldn't wait to be inside her later tonight, but in the meantime, he imposed his no-masturbating rule on himself, too.

After the hot-as-fuck phone sex though, he couldn't get Libby out of his mind. He really liked her. Even though they'd spent a good portion of their time together so far having sex, his gut told him they were compatible, not just in bed, but in life.

Granted, he'd thought the same thing once before with Veronica, and she'd burned him and left the scars behind. He'd spent the last three years trying to get on with his life. It didn't help that Libby had such a strange relationship with her parents, especially her mother. It made the hairs stand up on the back of his neck every time he remembered her telling him about them.

It's not the same, he told himself over and over. *She's not Veronica.* He'd begun to think he was simply being paranoid, but there were uncanny similarities between the two situations. Every time Jason had suggested meeting Veronica's parents, she'd blown him off. Libby was doing the same thing. Keeping him a secret. He would not play that game again. He'd been burned before. Not again.

When Jason knocked on the door to Libby's townhouse at seven, a cute blonde answered. He recognized her from Trent and Destiny's wedding. She smiled shyly and backed up to let him in. Her pale cheeks turned red. She licked her lips several times. "Libby will be right down. She's just finding her shoes."

"Good. Christa, right?"

She tucked a lock of pale blond hair behind her ear and nodded. "Yes. We met at the rehearsal dinner." She backed up toward the couch. "Come on in."

He followed her, glancing around at their townhouse. Their condo was two-stories with the kitchen and living room downstairs and probably two bedrooms upstairs. "I remember." He smiled at her. *Damn, she's shy.* "So, you live here with Libby?"

"Yes. I moved in after Destiny moved out. The rent is better than the place I was renting on my own." She pointed at the kitchen counter where he noticed three narrow vases, each containing a single rose. "The roses are very romantic. I wish someone would send me roses."

He frowned. Did she think he sent them to Libby? "I didn't send roses." He stepped closer to the counter and stared at them. "What made you think they were from me? Didn't they have a card?"

"Uh…no. You didn't send them?"

Footsteps made Jason lift his gaze to find Libby descending the stairs on the other side of the living room.

She was holding a pair of heels in her hand as she rushed toward him. "Sorry. Couldn't find my shoes." She held them up.

"No worries." He lifted a brow at her, wondering why she was so flustered.

"Uh, Libby," Christa said, "Jason says he didn't send the roses."

Libby's eyes widened. "Seriously?" She shifted her gaze toward the vases.

"No." He shook his head. There was no reason to be pissed. Especially since she had no idea who sent them. But his chest tightened, and he hoped to God there was nothing to read into it.

"Yikes." Christa winced.

Libby bit into her bottom lip and eased past him to touch one of the roses as if that would give her answers. "That's beyond weird."

"When did they come?" he asked.

"Saturday morning after I ran into you Friday night. Monday morning before I left for work. And this morning after I spoke to you. I just assumed..." Her voice trailed off.

"That's a lot of attention from a mysterious admirer," he pointed out, not wanting to sound accusatory. *This isn't her fault.*

"Maybe they're from your date Friday night?" Christa suggested.

"Eddie?" Libby turned back around. "That seems so unlikely. When he dropped me off, I gave him no indication I was interested in seeing him again. He hasn't tried to contact me, either."

Jason could feel his brow furrowing. He'd been in the Army, specifically with Delta Forces, long enough to scrutinize things in the civilian world with an irrationally doubtful eye. *They're just roses, Hatch. Not a bomb.*

LAYOVER

"Do you know what florist they're coming from?" he asked.

She shook her head. "I haven't paid attention."

"If you get another one, get the delivery driver's card. I'll go in and find out who's ordering them."

Libby swallowed. "You think it's a big deal?"

He lifted a brow. "I don't really care if it's a big deal or not. I'm not fond of some guy sending roses to the woman I'm dating." If he sounded cocky, he didn't care.

Libby smiled and reached out to wrap her small hand around his biceps. "I'll find out," she murmured before lifting onto her toes and kissing him briefly on the lips.

He blew out a breath as he cupped her face and held her gaze. He needed to shake off the uneasy feeling about her admirer and enjoy their evening.

Finally, Libby leaned down to put her heels on, and then she righted herself, blowing out a breath and smoothing her palms on her dress. She was breathtaking. The dress was white and fit snugly across her breasts and waist. It flared out over her butt, the looser material hanging halfway down her thighs.

She turned to Christa. "Not sure when I'll be back."

Christa smirked as she nodded. "Shocking."

Jason was slightly surprised at her snarky reaction since she'd barely managed to make eye contact with him. He stared at her for a second, wondering what Kraft might think of her. The man loved natural blondes. That was a fact. He might have even danced with her at the wedding reception. But Jason hadn't been paying close attention to anyone but Libby.

Christa continued. "I work early tomorrow, so I'll see you in a few days probably."

"'Kay." Libby leaned in and kissed her friend on the cheek. Afterward, she grabbed her small purse and a white sweater from the couch and met Jason's gaze.

95

"Ready?"

"Yep."

He glanced back at the roses before following her across the room. After stepping outside, he set a hand on the small of her back. When they reached his SUV, he opened the door and then gave her two seconds of struggling to climb into his car before he reached for her waist.

"Don't you dare." She shot him a glare.

He lifted his hands. "My bad."

She found her footing and climbed into the seat. When she met his gaze, she winced. "Sorry. I have a thing about letting people help me. I'm self-conscious about my size."

"Noted. Won't happen again. In public anyway." He smiled, hoping she would soften at his suggestion.

"Deal. If you want to lift me up to toss me onto your bed, that's fine. But I'm feisty otherwise."

He leaned in, cupped her face, and kissed her briefly on the lips. "I'm pretty sure my dick is harder now." He wasn't kidding. As he shut her door and rounded the hood, he adjusted his cock. Her determination turned him on.

After sitting in his seat and starting the SUV he turned to face her again. "You seem nervous. Are you worried about the roses?"

She sighed. "No. I just hung up with my mother. She can be very frustrating."

He tried to hide his internal flinch. "Ah. Right. Did she try to set you up with another guy?" he joked.

"It's not funny. That's her life's mission."

"Why don't you just tell her you're seeing someone?"

Libby squirmed. "Not yet." She didn't meet his gaze. Instead, she smoothed her skirt down over her thighs.

Jason stared at her for a few seconds, his fingers stiffening on the steering wheel. He didn't like this arrangement. It made him uncomfortable. How long could he push his concerns to the back of his mind? Surely this situation was nothing like what had happened with Veronica, he reminded himself. No way could the same thing happen to him twice.

Jason had one insecurity. Veronica had capitalized on it and made him feel like a complete fool. He would never let that happen again. Not for any woman.

Libby finally turned to face him. "I'm sorry. I know it's petty. But my mom is formidable. I don't want to rock the boat. Not this soon in our relationship. Can you please let it go for now?"

He nodded. Inside his head, warning bells were going off. More like sirens. But he forced them to quiet down. "For now. Not forever. But for now."

"Thank you."

Jason inhaled a deep breath and slowly let it out, chasing away his demons. Finally, he put the car in reverse and backed out of the spot. "How do you feel about Chinese food?"

She smiled. "Love it."

"Good. I found this amazing restaurant near my house. It's small and family-owned, and the food is excellent."

She perked up. "Perfect."

CHAPTER 13

Libby felt like a total bitch as they drove to the restaurant. Her mother had her completely flustered. She'd put off calling her all day, but when the woman started texting several times, she'd finally relented and answered. She'd regretted the choice in seconds.

"Libby. Finally. I've been trying to reach you. Why do you never answer your mother?" she'd whined. And then before Libby had been able to respond, "How was your date with Eddie? He seemed like such a nice guy when I met him." Maria Garcia had had a one-track mind tonight. She'd gone on and on, wanting every detail about Libby's date with Eddie. Libby had held her tongue and given her mother few details. It was none of her damn business.

Libby had put her off, knowing how pushy her mother could be. She'd told her she was too busy to think about dating. She had a lot of flights scheduled for this month because a few flight attendants were out sick. It was a lie, but she'd needed to come up with something.

The entire time she'd been thinking about Jason and his

insistence that she would not date other men. She understood. Perfectly. Of course, he wouldn't want her to date other people. The two of them had skipped casual and gone straight to extremely intimate.

But Libby had never had to juggle a secret boyfriend against her mother's constant string of blind dates. This situation was new, and it made Libby uncomfortable.

On top of everything else, Libby knew she'd pissed Jason off with her refusal to confront her mother. He didn't like it. They'd ridden to the restaurant mostly in silence. It wasn't until he parked and came around to open her door that he met her gaze again and smiled. His ire was gone. "You look amazing, by the way. I don't think I told you that."

Her cheeks heated. "Thank you. You look damn good yourself." He did. He was wearing black slacks and a black button-down shirt. The sleeves were rolled up. He'd shaved recently, and he smelled fantastic.

He filled the entire car door with his frame while he waited for her to remove her seatbelt, and then his hand landed on her thigh. Her breath hitched when he slid his fingers under her dress and eased them up between her legs. When he reached her sex, he nudged her thighs apart and stroked through her folds. "Good girl." He removed his hand far too soon and then sucked her arousal from his fingers.

She watched him, her heart racing at how damn hot this was. Fuck dinner. She would rather just go back to his place and have more wild kinky sex. They were good at that. So far, she couldn't be sure how good they were at dating. After the way he'd just teased her, and considering the promising look in his eyes, she imagined she would be squirming in her seat all through dinner.

Jason stepped back, offering her no assistance exiting his SUV, which earned him brownie points. The fact that he set his hand on the small of her back on the way into the restaurant pleased her even more.

After they were seated and had placed their order, he finally seemed to relax.

Libby blew out a breath. "I'm sorry I let my mother get to me earlier. I know it frustrates you." That much was obvious.

Jason sighed. "I'm confused is all. Why do you let your mother bother you so much? You're obviously self-sufficient and in control in most other aspects of your life. Why let her push you around?"

Libby nodded as she glanced down at the table, trying to figure out how to answer the burning question she herself didn't fully understand. "She's always been bossy. My entire life. She's a matriarch. Even my father lets her run the show. She dictated a lot of what everyone in the house did while I was growing up. At some point, I knew I wanted something different for myself when I moved out on my own."

"And did you accomplish that?"

"Yes. I worked my ass off to put myself through college even though I had no idea at the time what I wanted to do with my life. I coveted that degree mostly because my mother thought it was frivolous and unnecessary. She refused to pay for it."

Jason frowned. "You paid for everything on your own?"

"Mostly. My father slipped me money as often as he could, but I worked a lot of hours waiting tables to cover most of my expenses. I'm proud of my accomplishment, and I have a nice diploma from UT Dallas to show for it, but along the way, I met Christa and Destiny through mutual friends and grew more interested in becoming a flight attendant."

"Nothing wrong with that. I hear it's decent money."

She shrugged. "It's okay. More importantly, it allows me to travel a lot. I get to see so many places, and being out of town often keeps my mother off my back."

The waitress arrived with their meals. After she wandered away, Jason spoke again. "You can't live your entire life letting her dictate your every move." His expression was one of concern, probably more for himself than her. *Understandable.* What did it say about her that she let her mother get under her skin?

"I know," she murmured. "Christa tells me the same thing often. And I get it. I'm just not ready to confront her."

"Look, I'm trying to understand. Not going to lie; it bothers me. On the other hand, we haven't been seeing each other very long. If I'm reading you correctly, you're thinking why rock that boat for no good reason. It makes sense that you'd rather wait until we've known each other longer before you talk to your parents. I'll give you that. Not forever, but for now."

"Thank you. You said exactly what I'm thinking. Can we just see where things go for a while?"

"Absolutely." He gave her one of his gorgeous smiles and then speared a piece of broccoli from his beef broccoli.

She took a bite of her chicken fried rice and then sipped her iced tea. "How has work been?"

"Good. Busy. Jake has more jobs coming in than we can cover. It can sometimes be feast or famine when running a consulting firm, but considering how fast technology is changing, I don't see computer programming dying off any time in my life."

"True."

"I got together with several of the guys from work Tuesday night. Poker night. Kraft's house."

"That's cool. Do you do that every Tuesday?"

"Not always. Random days. Four guys from work. Me, Kraft, Sweets, and Tank." He sounded animated as he spoke of his coworkers.

"Trent mentioned them to me once when he came to see

Destiny. You explained Kraft's name to me, but what's the origin story for the others?" She smiled, lifting a brow.

"Tank is actually my boss. I told you about him. His real name is Jake Robinson. His nickname is self-explanatory. Big guy. Broad. Tall. Muscular. Sweets, on the other hand, that's a funny story. The guy's idea of unwinding includes making delicious pastries, cakes, and any other dessert you can think of. He's hilarious when he puts on an apron and pulls out the flour. Apparently, his team gave him shit until they realized they wouldn't get to devour his sweets if they didn't stop making fun of him. After that, the name began to hold great reverence."

Libby laughed. "And these guys all work with you?"

"Yep. Jake snagged each of us when we got out of the army. Kraft and I were on the same Delta Team."

"Wow. Impressive. I didn't realize you'd been on a special forces team."

He shrugged. "No big deal. I'm not sure why I even mentioned it."

"It *is* a big deal. You must have done some incredibly dangerous things over the years."

He shrugged again and then winked at her. "It's in the past."

"Got it. What's Sweets' real name?" She'd rather not burn these nicknames into her mind. It was too confusing.

"Bracken Turner. Great guy."

She shot him a cocky grin. "Are they single?" she asked.

He lifted a brow, smirking. "Why? One dominant military guy isn't enough for you?"

She chuckled. "Asking for a friend. Several of them, actually."

He laughed. "I don't think you can use that phrase when you really mean it. But yes. They're single. It's tough dating while serving in the military. Lots of women think it's romantic—you included—but it's hard to build a relationship and even harder to keep it going."

"Yeah, I'm guilty of thinking it would be romantic. Little did I know it would knock me on my ass." She smiled.

He set his fork down, leaned over the table, and cupped her face. "I love knowing I knocked you on your ass. I also love that I ran into you again now that I'm more available. Am I still attractive to you now that I'm not active?" he teased.

"Very." She tipped her face into his palm, caught his thumb with her mouth, and sucked it in between her lips.

He groaned. "That was hot the first time you did it, and it's even hotter now."

She released his thumb with a pop. "As I recall, you didn't give me a choice the first time. And you're right, it was damn hot. I think that was the moment I knew for certain you were going to rock my world and leave me spinning out of control."

Jason stroked her cheek and then sat back. "You're making it hard for me to care about finishing this meal."

She squirmed in her seat, squeezing her legs together on the bench across from him. She liked the intimacy of the booth, but part of her wished they'd sat on the same side. If he had her pinned against the wall, there was a chance his hand could be on her thigh right now, teasing her skin mercilessly.

She bit into her bottom lip and tried to control her beating heart. There was no hope, however. Every time she was with Jason, he had this power over her. He made her body sing with arousal. Was this a passing thing that would burn itself out in a few weeks or months? Or did it have staying power?

She wasn't ready or able to face those questions, and she hoped it didn't matter for now. Time would tell her how serious this was. As long as Jason gave her that time, she would use it to figure out how on earth she might go about informing her mother that she was dating a white guy.

The problem was that the thought of ever finding

someone who could make her feel as alive as Jason did was unimaginable. They had a rare connection, and she knew he felt it too.

Why does everything have to be so complicated?

CHAPTER 14

One week later...

Libby smiled as she turned her phone on and saw a text from Jason.

Hey, baby girl, I know you're traveling today, but I wasn't sure what time you would get home. I wondered if I could see you when you get back in town.

I wish. She sighed. She was supposed to have returned to Dallas earlier this evening, but instead, her flight had been delayed and she was now stuck spending the night in Denver because she'd worked too many hours and timed out.

Disappointed, Libby pulled her overnight bag through the airport and took a shuttle to the hotel. She waited until she was in her room before she texted him back.

I hope I'm not waking you. I know it's late. I got stuck in Denver.

Flights were delayed. I won't be home until tomorrow afternoon. I just got to my hotel.

Seconds later, her phone rang and her heart beat faster as she answered. "Hey," she said, her voice breathy. She kicked off her shoes as she put the phone on speaker so she could get out of her uniform.

"Hey there. Sorry you got delayed."

"Yeah. Me too. It happens. I'd rather it didn't happen on a night you wanted to see me." She was really disappointed. She'd seen him three nights in the past week, but it hadn't seemed like enough. She found herself thinking about him all the time when they weren't together. She'd also started traveling with her vibrator, although lately, it didn't even take the added battery-powered toy to get her off when she closed her eyes and thought of Jason.

"You miss me," he pointed out, his voice teasing.

"Yeah."

"What are you wearing?" His voice dipped lower, softer, sexier.

She glanced down as she dropped her skirt. Her blouse was already on the bed. "My bra and panties."

"Really? Have you been stripping while we speak?"

"Yes." The phone was sitting on the mattress. She cupped her breasts and squeezed them, moaning unintentionally.

"Naughty girl," he admonished. "I want to see."

A second later, her phone buzzed, indicating he was switching them to FaceTime.

She released her breasts and tapped the screen to accept the call, leaning over it so that her face came into view. She gave him an evil grin.

"Don't tease me, baby girl. Pick up the phone and show me what you're wearing."

She lifted the cell and slowly tipped it toward her bare shoulder, giving him a glimpse of her bra strap.

"More, little one. I need to see you. Since you're not in my bed tonight, I'm going to have to settle for the next best thing. A show. Do as you're told or my palm will be the first thing that touches you the next time I see you. A hard spanking will teach you not to tease me."

Libby's face heated as she lowered the phone slowly, letting him see her lace bra and then the dip of her belly before she hovered over the triangle at the front of her panties. She shivered as she watched herself revealed to him on the screen.

The last time she'd been on FaceTime with Jason, he had watched her face while she masturbated. He had not seen her naked. The thought of displaying herself like this made her nipples stiffen. It was naughty, just like he'd called her.

She brought the phone slowly back to her face, licking her lips.

"Good girl. Climb up on the bed for me."

She did as he told her, holding the phone with one hand.

"How many pillows are at the head of the bed, little one?"

She glanced over her shoulder. "It's a hotel. I don't know why they think people need this many pillows, but there are about six."

"Good. Situate them so you can lean back, but put one between your legs and prop your phone against it so I can see all of you."

She swallowed. *Can I do this? Perform for him through the phone?* She'd never even taken a nude picture of herself, let alone stripped for a man while he watched through the phone. He could ruin her with this if he wanted to.

"Libby... You're hesitating."

"It's so taboo, Sir."

His breath hitched when she called him Sir. She knew he

liked it when she spoke to him with such reverence. He'd never instructed her to call him Sir. She'd simply done it on her own any time he was dominating her. He was certainly dominating her now.

"I promise I'm not recording you, baby girl. I would never violate your trust that way. This is for no one but me. No one else will ever see it. When we hang up, it won't even exist."

She bit her lip as she held his gaze through the phone. "Yes, Sir." She was still hesitant as she rearranged the pillows behind her and then brought one down between her legs. By the time she had the phone propped up against the pillow, she'd calmed her racing heart somewhat.

The view on the screen was smokin' hot. She parted her legs farther, giving him a full shot of the black lace triangle that covered her pussy.

"That's a girl. So pretty. Set your hands on your thighs, little one. Stroke the skin alongside your panties."

She did as he told her, watching herself on the screen. It was like watching an erotic film or porn. Except it was far more authentic because she was truly enjoying herself.

"Are your panties wet, baby girl?"

"Yes, Sir. Soaked." She drew a finger over the top, moaning as she flicked over her clit.

"Naughty girl. Don't get ahead of yourself. Do as you're told."

"Yes, Sir."

"Pull that lace to one side so I can see your pussy."

She was shaking as she obeyed this command, and she gasped as her swollen, wet lips came into view. This was so erotic. She'd never watched herself masturbate.

"Stroke a finger through your folds now. Slowly."

She held the lace with one hand and touched herself with the other. Her breath hitched at the contact, as if she weren't the one touching herself.

"Do you have a vibrator with you, baby girl?" His voice was gravelly now. He was as aroused as her. She could only see his face, but she imagined his hand was wrapped around his cock.

Her face heated again as she admitted what a horny girl she'd been. "Yes, Sir," she murmured.

"What's that, little one? I couldn't hear you."

She drew in a breath. "I brought a bullet with me, Sir."

"You are so naughty, aren't you?" He was smiling.

"Yes. Since I met you."

"You didn't travel with a vibrator before you met me?"

"No." She shook her head.

"Go get it. And remove your bra and panties. Come right back. You have thirty seconds."

She hesitated, swallowing. Finally, she lifted one leg over the pillow prop and slid from the bed. With shaky fingers, she found the little pink bullet in her overnight bag, shrugged out of her panties, and unfastened her bra. It fell to the floor as she climbed back onto the bed and returned to the same position. She held the bullet up for him to see, blocking his view of her pussy.

"Good girl. Now let me see you. Spread open for me. Angle the camera so I can see your sweet tits, too."

She adjusted the screen and leaned back, her chest heaving. This was so damn erotic.

"So sexy. Pull your pussy lips open for me."

She tucked the bullet in her palm and obeyed him, falling under his spell so easily. She knew he would make it worthwhile.

"Turn the vibrator onto the highest setting and push it up inside you, baby girl."

She was panting as she turned it on, and she gritted her teeth as she slid it into her. She moaned. Nothing was touching her clit, but God, she was so close.

"How does that feel, baby girl?"

"So good, Sir."

"I bet you need to come, don't you?"

"Yes, Sir." *So badly.*

"I want you to play with your clit. I want to watch you come. But there's a catch."

She sucked in a breath. "What's the catch, Sir?" *How could this get any more erotic?*

"You have three minutes. If you can't come in that time, you have to stop and you don't get to come tonight."

Her eyes widened. "Sir…"

"The timer is starting right now. You better get to work."

She hesitated. She'd never come that fast before. Or maybe she had when she'd been with him. Alone? Never.

"Libby…" he warned.

She leaned back, closed her eyes, and stroked her clit. She was so aroused that even that slight touch informed her she just might win this challenge. She held the hood back with one hand, gathered her wetness with the other, and rubbed her clit, flicking it and pinching it. She imagined her fingers were his the entire time.

God, it felt so good. She lost track of time, but flinched when he spoke. "One minute left, baby girl. Come for me. Show me how turned on you are."

Her clit swelled further at his words, and she picked up the pace, biting into her lower lip and squeezing her eyes tighter. *So close. So damn close.* Her ears started ringing as she reached higher. Her legs stiffened. She gasped when she reached the peak and finally went over the edge.

Panting, she kept rubbing herself through the waves of pleasure, not opening her eyes until she finally too sensitive to continue.

She blinked at Jason. He was smiling. "That was the sexiest thing I've ever seen."

"Thank you, Sir." She picked up the phone with shaking hands and rolled onto her side, holding the cell so that he only saw her face now. With her free hand, she pulled the bullet out of her and turned it off. She dragged her knees up toward her chest, squeezing them together.

"You're exquisite, little one."

She smiled at him. "That was so hot."

"Not as good as having you in my bed, but a close second."

"Yes." She was still breathing heavily.

"You land tomorrow afternoon?" he asked. "What time can I expect you at my house?"

She winced. "You can't. Not tomorrow. I have to go to my parents' house for dinner."

His face tightened slightly. "Ah. I see."

She bit her lip. She wanted to apologize. She wanted to have the kind of parents who would welcome her bringing a date. Any date. Even a white date. But she didn't. And saying anything to him would just make her sound lame.

"Come over afterward?" he asked, his eyelids lifting.

"Yes." She smiled, blowing out a breath, relieved he wasn't going to make a big deal out of this. "I'd love to."

"Great. Don't wear panties." His eyes danced.

She giggled. "Of course not, Sir." He didn't look angry, but she knew she was pushing him every time the subject of her parents came up.

She watched as he inhaled slowly, his face morphing into a more serious expression. "Have any more roses come, Libby?"

She shook her head. "Not since the fourth one."

He nodded, but his frustration was palpable. She'd done as he'd asked and gotten the florist's information, and Jason had gone into the shop to speak to the manager. Unfortunately, all the roses were purchased over the phone using a prepaid Visa card. It had been difficult to pull that much information out of the manager, but Libby didn't figure many people turned Jason down when he got in their space.

"Maybe whoever it is has given up," she suggested, though she only half-believed those words herself. It was mind-boggling. She found herself frequently wracking her brain once again, trying to imagine who might be essentially stalking her.

The bummer was that she'd dated several men of her mother's choosing lately, and though she'd felt no connection to any of them, she found it unlikely one of them was so into her that he was sending roses.

She closed her eyes against the shudder that shook her body. If one of her recent dates wanted to see her again, why didn't he just text or call? How was it helpful to send anonymous roses?

"Libby…"

She smiled at the warning tone in Jason's voice.

"Stop thinking about the roses, baby girl. I'm sorry I brought it up. Let it go from your mind now."

"Yes, Sir."

"Good girl. Sleep well, little one. I'll see you tomorrow."

"Good night, Sir." She ended the call and closed her eyes, taking a deep breath. Shaking all thoughts of her anonymous suitor from her mind, she focused on Jason instead. She was really falling hard for this guy. *What the hell am I going to do about my parents?*

CHAPTER 15

Libby was exhausted when she arrived at her parents' house. After working all day, the last thing she wanted to do was make nice with her mother. She'd much rather be at Jason's house. Preferably naked and on her knees. Or handcuffed to his bed... Or over his knee...

She would find a way to get this dinner over with fast and get to his house.

She opened the front door warily, entered, and made her way through the front room toward the voices coming from the kitchen at the back of the house.

When she stepped inside, she froze. Her mother was at the stove stirring something. Her father was leaning against the island with a beer in his hand. And holy mother of God, Eddie was sitting on one of the bar stools.

Eddie was the first to spot her, and he beamed as he rose from the stool and came across the room toward her. "Hey there." He leaned in close and kissed her cheek. "How was work?"

She blinked at him. What the hell was he doing at her

parents' house and why was he acting like they were a couple and she'd known he would be here?

"Hey, honey," her mother tossed over her shoulder as she continued to stir. "Fun surprise, huh? I knew you'd been working a lot of hours lately, and I hated imposing on a night you could have been on a date, so I invited Eduardo." She turned around, smiling wide as if she'd just pulled off the best surprise party ever. "This way, your father and I get to spend some time with you, and you're not even missing out on a date night." She clapped her hands together with incredible satisfaction.

Eddie looked quite pleased also. "I was so glad your mother called. I told her our schedules haven't meshed lately. I assume you've gotten my roses though?" Was he smirking?

Surely she was imagining things. She stared at him, unable to imagine what she might say next.

Her father came to her side and kissed her forehead. "Good to see you, Libby."

Her mom turned back to stirring, speaking again over her shoulder. "Libby, would you mind taking the bread to the dining room? The stew is almost ready. I'll bring it in soon."

Has the entire world gone mad? Did anyone in the room realize she had yet to speak?

Libby's father handed her a basket filled with steaming bread and waved her toward the dining room with a wink. As if he was conspiring to give her time alone with Eddie.

Yep. The world's gone mad.

Libby felt like she was out of her body as she shuffled to the dining room, breadbasket in one hand, Eddie right behind her. She was also furious, both with her mother and with Eddie. How dare he think this would be appropriate.

He set his palm on her lower back, making her shudder as she dropped the bread on the table. "Sorry I haven't called. I was out of town for several days, and I knew you were working a busy schedule."

She spun around fast and took a step back to get his hand off her. "I didn't expect you to call at all. I thought we agreed we didn't really have chemistry." They had discussed this. Using those words. She'd learned to be careful with the men she dated. If it wasn't going to work, she made that clear the moment they dropped her off. She didn't like to lead people on. It was one thing to date a string of men her mother set her up with, but there was no way she was going to go out with someone twice if she wasn't feeling it.

Eddie waved a hand through the air, dismissing her comment. "We only went on the one date. I thought it went well. We hardly got the chance to get to know each other in the noisy bar."

It hadn't been just noisy. Eddie had brought her to a birthday party for one of his friends. She hadn't known a single person there. It was kind of rude for a first date. And she'd found him to be presumptuous and cocky as fuck.

He'd also touched her too often. His hand had always been on her arm or back or even her thigh. She hadn't liked it much when they first arrived, and she'd liked it even less after running into Jason.

She rubbed her forehead with two fingers, closing her eyes. Visions of how Jason had touched her on their first dance and then in his hotel room less than half an hour later made her almost laugh. She'd never get enough of Jason's touch. But Eddie? *Just no.*

She finally took a deep breath and met his gaze. She needed to nip this in the bud. "This isn't going to work, Eddie."

"Why not?" He looked perplexed, though she thought it was feigned. "Are you seeing someone else?"

Fuck. She needed to dodge that question in case her

mother walked in. "That's not what matters, Eddie. I'm just not interested."

He smiled and had the audacity to reach out and stroke her cheek. "Well, I'm here now. Let's enjoy the evening and see how it goes."

Her mother walked in with the steaming pot in her hand moments later, her father following.

Her mother's smile was huge. "Let's all sit." She set the pot down and then clapped her hands together one time in that annoying way she often did to punctuate her words.

Libby stared at Eddie for several seconds, shocked by his tenacity. The man pulled out a chair for her, for fuck's sake. Libby sat, her heart pounding. What the hell was she going to do?

Her mother started rambling, asking Eddie a thousand questions as if the two of them had arrived to announce their engagement. Eddie answered every question as if he were the poster child for politeness. Libby wanted to stab his fake self with her fork.

And since when did her mother make stew and serve it with bread? Since never. Libby didn't listen very carefully to the ridiculous small talk because her ears were ringing, but she caught the edge of a conversation about the fact that Eddie was so Americanized—her mother's exact word—that he preferred American cooking.

Libby's brows raised. Apparently, it was okay for the man to be American as long as his parents hailed from Guatemala. Libby felt like she was watching a job interview. Eddie was being interviewed as an appropriate suitor, and he was passing with flying colors. No one seemed to care what Libby thought.

Her father glanced at her several times. He even looked a bit chagrined as if he realized this situation was all kinds of fucked-up and wanted to apologize with his eyes, but the man didn't say a word.

As soon as it seemed even marginally reasonable, Libby wiped her lips, dropped her napkin, and pushed to standing. "I can't stay. I have to work early tomorrow. Thanks for dinner, Mamá." She nodded at her father and then reluctantly at Eddie and turned to head for the front door.

"I'll walk you out," Eddie stated, jumping up to rush behind her.

Libby walked fast, unamused to say the least. She forced Eddie to nearly jog to keep up with her as she stepped out the front door and rushed toward her car.

She was shaking as she unlocked the car with her fob.

Eddie set his hand on the roof, blocking her. "Hey. I guess this wasn't such a great idea, huh?"

She rolled her eyes and cocked her head. "Ya think?"

He shrugged, looking irritated. "When your mom called, I assumed you had spoken favorably about me to her. That's why I came."

"Well, I didn't speak of you at all, Eddie. She dreams this shit up on her own."

He had the decency to at least wince. "Okay, but I still think we should go out again sometime. We had a good time that night. My friends loved you."

His friends couldn't have loved her. She barely spoke to them, and they barely acknowledged her.

"Eddie, there's no other way for me to say this. I'm not interested. It's not going to happen between us." Was this guy dense?

He patted the top of her car. "Well, I disagree. I think you should consider another date with me. I'll call you in a few days."

She groaned. "I'm not going to change my mind."

He shrugged. "We'll see. We make a good couple. My

parents and your parents are friends. A relationship between us is so tidy. They would all be thrilled. Win-win. Plus, I'm attracted to you. You're smoking hot." He reached out to stroke her cheek, grinning.

She swatted his hand away and then shoved his body back a few feet so she could climb into the car and slam the door. Without another glance—because seriously, he didn't deserve one—she drove away.

She was so fucking pissed. Her hands were shaking on the steering wheel. She'd meant to go straight to Jason's house, but now she didn't think that was a good idea. Not in this state of mind—furious. Besides, what the hell was she going to say to him? He was going to be equally irate. Rightfully so.

When am I going to grow a spine?

She headed back to her townhouse, and when she got there, she grabbed her overnight bag from the back seat and went inside.

Christa was on the couch watching television and painting her nails. She looked up, surprised. "What happened? I thought you weren't coming home tonight."

Libby groaned and dropped down on the armchair. "My mother happened. I'm too angry to go over to Jason's now."

Christa cringed. "What did she do?"

"She fucking set me up with Eddie again."

"The guy you were with the night you ran into Jason?"

Libby nodded. "Yep."

"What do you mean she set you up? Was he there at your parents' house?"

"Yep," she repeated.

"Ouch. What did you do?"

"I gave Eddie a piece of my mind, ate my damn meal in silence, and then bailed."

"And you haven't told Jason…"

Libby rubbed a hand down her face and shook her head.

"He's not going to like it."

"I'm sure, but you have to be honest with him, or you're going to make it worse."

"Yeah, I know." Libby sighed. "I couldn't go over there like this though. My blood is boiling. He's not the right person for me to vent about my mom's blind dates."

"True. Good point."

"Ugh. I need to text him at least." There was no way Libby was going to lie about any of this. It wouldn't help her out at all. She pulled out her phone and texted.

Hey. Shit hit the fan with my mom tonight. I'm back at my place. I didn't want to come over there angry.

A few moments later, she got a response.

I'm sorry about your mom. Come over anyway. I'll make you forget.

He added an evil-faced emoji that made her giggle.

One thing was for sure—if she didn't go over to Jason's, her mother would have kind of gotten what she wanted. That infuriated Libby even more. She decided to go.

Okay. But we need to talk first. I'll be there soon.

First before what?

He added yet another evil-faced emoji.

"You're smiling," Christa pointed out.

Libby put her phone away. "Yeah. Okay. I guess I'm going over there. Wish me luck." She shoved off the couch, grabbed her bag, and headed out the door once again.

"Good luck," Christa called out.

CHAPTER 16

Jason met Libby at the door, touching her back as she passed under his arm. After closing the door, he grabbed her around the waist and pulled her into his arms.

He wanted to look into her eyes and gauge her emotions. The text conversation had been off. He'd have gotten a better bead on her feelings if she'd called.

Cupping her face, he looked into her eyes.

She met his gaze but then dropped her head and set her forehead against his chest. "Ugh. Let me tell you what happened."

"Okay." He slid a hand to hers and lured her toward the kitchen. For the first time, he sorely wished he had a sofa. They had two choices—bar stools in the kitchen or his bed. "Can I get you a drink?" he asked as he pulled out a bar stool for her.

She hopped up onto it and sighed. "Water would be great."

He grabbed a bottle from the fridge and handed it to her before taking the other stool. "Tell me what happened." He reached for her hand and held it loosely, nerves starting to make his pulse pick up. She was really off.

"Remember that guy I was out with when we ran into each other?"

"Yes. Eddie." How could he forget? *And fuck me, but I don't like where this is going.*

"Well, my mom invited him to her house for dinner."

Jason's eyes popped wide. Even though he should have seen this coming, he was still shocked. "And..." *Please tell me you left.*

She pulled her hand out of his and groaned before setting both hands on her head. "I was caught off-guard. So fucking stunned, I didn't know what to do."

"So you told your mom to stop meddling in your life, and you left." He knew he was wrong, but damn, he wanted to be right.

Her shoulders dropped and she shook her head. "No. I did tell Eddie that I wasn't the least bit interested in him and never would be. It hardly made him flinch. The man is convinced we would make a perfect couple. It's like he couldn't hear a word I said."

Jason stared at her, trying to process what she was saying. There was no reason to be mad at her. She hadn't really done anything wrong. Except not stand up to her mother. Which was everything.

He stood, needing to pace and think. And take several breaths.

After a few moments, Libby spoke again. "Oh, and he's the one who sent the roses."

Jason spun to face her, fisting his hands at his sides. "Seriously?"

She nodded. Her expression was drawn.

"Jesus," he muttered.

She drew in a long breath. "Look, I knew you would be mad. I almost didn't come over. I considered not telling you at all. But I didn't want there to be any secrets between us. I went to my mom's. She ambushed me. I told Eddie to take a hike. I left."

"But you also sat at the table and ate dinner," he accused.

She lowered her gaze and sighed. "Yes. If you want to call it eating. I stabbed at my food for about fifteen minutes while thinking about how I was going to get out of there."

A war was taking place in his head. On the one hand, she'd told him exactly what happened. On the other hand, he still thought she was stringing him along. "I'm gonna be honest, Libby. I don't like this. I don't like that you're lying to your parents, and I certainly don't like that some guy is stalking you."

She pulled in a breath and slid off the stool. How the woman could make jeans and a fitted white T-shirt look sexy was beyond him, but she always managed to make him take notice. Even now. Even though he was off-kilter and so was she.

She took a step back. "I'm gonna go."

He jerked. "Go? Why?"

She turned and started shuffling toward the front door, speaking as she walked. "Because I'm stressed, Jason. My evening was shit. I have some fucking guy basically stalking me, and the man I really like is more interested in what my stupid parents think than any other single thing. I want to go home and sleep."

He jogged toward her to close the distance, wrapping an arm gently around her middle before she reached the door and pulling her back against his chest. He rocked her back and forth and set his lips near her ear. "You're right. I'm sorry. Don't go."

She blew out a breath, but she was stiff in his arms.

He brushed her hair from her neck and kissed her, inhaling her scent while forcing himself not to get carried away. He was at least as nervous as Libby. The last thing he wanted was for her to leave tonight. "I overreacted," he whispered.

She leaned her head against him. "Jason, you have to let up about my parents. We've been dating like ten days. I know it's intense, and I really like you, but I'm not going to declare my undying love for someone to my mom this early in a relationship."

He hated to admit she was right, and he knew his insecurities were clouding his judgment. *She's not Veronica,* he told himself yet again. It was hard to remember that when every time he turned around, the similarities between the two of them piled up.

"You're right," he admitted. "Please stay."

She turned around in his embrace and tipped her head back, her hands on his hips. "One condition."

"Anything."

"My brain is on overload. I'm exhausted. Can we just sleep?"

He smiled. "Of course." Relief flooded him. For the first time since he could remember, he'd give anything to have this woman in his bed, in his arms. Even if they didn't have sex. "One condition," he parroted, offering her a sly smile.

"Anything," she repeated.

"I get to wake you up with my mouth on your pussy."

She smiled broader. "Who could turn down a deal like that?"

He released her long enough to grab her bag and then they headed down the hallway to the master bedroom.

She entered his bathroom and shut the door, reemerging five minutes later. In the meantime, he'd stripped down to his boxers and climbed under the covers. She padded toward him in the dark, removed her shoes and jeans, and then unfastened her bra and pulled it off under her shirt. She dropped both on the floor and climbed into the bed.

He would have rather had her naked, but he would take anything. The moment she was under the covers, he spooned her, wrapping one arm under her breasts and kissing her neck.

She sighed, relaxing into his embrace. "Thank you," she murmured.

"Any time, baby girl. I know it might seem like it, but I don't think our relationship is based on sex. Do we have amazing sex? Yes. Is it mandatory? No. I just love having you in my arms."

She snuggled closer, he hoped in agreement.

CHAPTER 17

Libby smiled as she slowly came awake. The sun was just starting to peek around the edges of the blinds, and true to his word, Jason was between her legs, the covers shoved down the bed.

She was still wearing her panties, but he had his arms hooked under her legs and was kissing the sensitive skin of her inner thighs.

She fisted the sheets at her sides and arched her chest when he scraped his teeth along the edge of her panties.

"I love that sound, little one." He nosed her pussy through the silk material, causing her to groan again. In one swift movement, he drew back, grabbed the hem of her panties, and tugged them off her body. Two seconds later, he was back between her legs, his tongue lapping at her folds.

She arched again. He could play her body like no man ever had, and she loved being reminded of it often.

"Push your shirt up over your tits, baby girl. Play with your nipples for me."

She shivered at the demand but somehow managed to haul her T-shirt up toward her neck and then cupped her breasts.

He was kissing her pussy, nibbling it, really. All over. Driving her arousal higher by the second. "Please..."

He flicked his tongue over her clit. "Pinch your nipples, baby. I want to see them stiffen."

She obeyed his command, whimpering as she plucked the swollen buds.

"Good girl. Keep playing with them while I get you off."

She'd never done anything like this, but it was heady. Granted, she's masturbated for him on the phone, but this was different. She was fondling herself while he watched. And it felt so good.

He sucked her clit in hard, making her dig her heels into the mattress. When he released it, he flicked his tongue over it rapidly.

As her arousal rose, she pinched her nipples harder. They were going to be sore later. She didn't care. It was worth it right now.

When his teeth scraped the hood of her clit, she cried out. "Jason." She was panting, shaking with the need to come.

Suddenly he stopped, releasing her pussy.

Her eyes went wide as he leaned over her body and tugged the bedside table drawer open. He was back moments later, kneeling between her legs, rolling a condom down his cock.

His gaze was on hers. Possessive. Serious. Demanding. Hot as hell. And then he dropped onto his forearms while she continued to stroke her breasts. He thrust into her without warning, taking her breath away. Her eyes rolled back as he kissed her.

It was hard to return the kiss since her brain cells were only firing messages to her pussy, but he teased her lips open with his tongue and then stroked it along hers.

She could taste herself on his lips and tongue.

He waited until she was squirming beneath him to pull out and thrust back into her.

She moaned into his mouth, making him smile against her as he released her lips and met her gaze. "Damn, you are sexy." He held her gaze as he thrust again. And again.

She tipped her head back finally, unable to maintain eye contact as she neared the edge of sanity. And then, she was right there, holding her breath, willing the orgasm back a few more seconds. God, she loved that space, the time between when she reached the edge and when she fell off the cliff. That delicious point where she teetered before falling.

As her orgasm took over, Jason thrust harder until he too stiffened and came deep inside her.

When they were both spent, he hovered over her several more moments, kissing her face and neck and lips. Finally, he pulled out and dropped to a hip beside her, one leg between hers, his hand on her belly. He was struggling to catch his breath. "Good morning."

She giggled as she smoothed a hand over his forearm. "Yes, it is."

An hour later, they were both showered and dressed, sitting at his kitchen island.

"You're off today?" Jason asked as he handed her coffee.

"Yeah." She groaned as she tipped her head back and stared at the ceiling. "I'll go talk to my mom. That stunt last night was out of line."

"What about Eddie?" Jason furrowed his brow. "You think he got the hint?"

She sighed. "I don't know. We'll see."

Her phone rang on the counter, and she reached for it when she saw Christa's name on the screen. "Hey. You're up early."

"Yeah. There was a delivery for you. I dragged myself out of bed to answer the door."

Libby stiffened. "Shit. It's not even eight."

"Don't I know it."

"What was it?"

"No idea. A package. It had to be signed for. I set it on the table, but I thought you'd want to know. Especially with the mysterious roses and all."

"Shit. I forgot to tell you the roses came from Eddie. Surely he wouldn't send a package this morning after our confrontation last night. I made myself super clear."

"I could open it if you want?"

Jason reached for the phone and took it from Libby. "Christa, don't open it. I'll come over and check it out." He handed the phone back to Libby, kissed her forehead, and left the room in a hurry.

"Shit," Libby muttered into the phone.

Christa sighed dramatically. "He's gone all Rambo on you, hasn't he?"

"It would seem so."

"That's so romantic."

"I'm not sure about that. It's probably overkill. It's just a package. We don't even know who it's from yet."

"There's no name on the box. Other than yours, I mean."

"Guess we'll be there in a bit then."

"See you soon."

CHAPTER 18

Jason followed Libby to her townhouse, doing his best to talk himself off the precarious ledge. There was no reason to get freaked out about a package. Hell, maybe Libby had ordered something and forgotten about it. Could be anything. There was no reason to believe it was from Eddie and that he refused to accept no for an answer.

When they arrived, he followed Libby inside. Christa was in the kitchen, sipping coffee. She pointed at the box on the table.

Jason had his hands fisted at his sides as he stared at it. Libby stepped in front of him and flattened her palms on his chest. "I'm sure it's no big deal." Her words were soft. She was trying to placate him.

He met her gaze, frowning. "I just got out of the Army. Nothing in my world is no big deal. Let's judge that after I open it." He narrowed his gaze. "You don't mind if I open it, do you?"

She shook her head. "Not at all. But I also don't think it warrants the stress you feel, as if it's a bomb."

He ran a hand down his face. She was right. Part of him

was just pissed that this guy wouldn't leave her alone. If the box was from Eddie, there was a good chance Jason would hunt the guy down, and he was in no mood to be kind about it. Enough was enough.

Libby stepped back and turned to face the box. It was long and flat. Like a shirt box but larger. She lifted it. "It doesn't weigh much."

Jason took it from her hands. "May I?"

She nodded.

Christa sat across from them, her hand on her chest. He was pretty sure she was about to swoon, and it had nothing to do with the box. Her gaze was on him.

He took out his pocket knife and ran it along the sides to cut the tape. When the lid was freed, he pulled it off. He saw delicate tissue paper first, and then Libby reached over and parted the white paper to reveal black material and a note on top.

Her fingers were shaking as she lifted the note first and opened it.

Jason unapologetically leaned over her shoulder to read along while Libby read it out loud.

Libertad, I'm so sorry about our misunderstanding. I shouldn't have shown up last night without making sure you knew I was coming. It was insensitive of me. When I saw this dress, I thought of you. Please accept it as my way of apologizing. Hopefully, you can forgive me and let me take you out on a real date this weekend. No friends. No parents. Just the two of us.

There was a good chance flames were coming out of Jason's head. "Is this guy fucking for real?"

Libby lifted the silk dress out of the box and held it up. "My God."

"That's more like lingerie," Christa commented. She leaned

forward and picked up the tag. "Shit. This cost a fortune. Look at the brand."

The brand meant nothing to Jason, but the fact that some other man had thought it appropriate to buy his woman a gift —let alone something this fucking sexy—made his blood boil.

Libby spun it around. The back was bare. She wouldn't even be able to wear a bra with it. Finally, she dropped it into the box and put the lid back on. She lifted her gaze to Jason. "I'll talk to him this morning."

He shook his head. "Not a chance. You're done talking to him. I'll talk to him. Do you have his address? Give me every piece of information you have on him."

Libby drew in a breath. "I don't have his address. Just a phone number. I could get more information from my mom, but not without explaining why. Besides, you can't confront him, Jason."

"Why the fuck not? The guy is stalking you."

"He's right," Christa added. Thank God someone besides Jason saw the seriousness of this situation.

Libby rubbed her forehead. "If you confront him, he'll figure out I'm involved with you and tell my parents."

Jason groaned as he rolled his head back. "Libby, this is crazy. Someone has to tell this guy to fuck off and make sure he hears it loud and clear this time. He's not going to stop this nonsense. It's not safe. He's unbalanced."

"That's putting it mildly," Christa added. "He's a lunatic."

Jason nodded. He hadn't wanted to put it so bluntly and risk angering Libby more. "How about if you go talk to your mom while I go talk to Eddie? Let's put an end to this."

Libby chewed on her bottom lip and then shook her head. "Please. Let *me* handle it."

He stared at her. His brain was screaming at him to get out of this relationship right now. It was moving into territory he couldn't stomach. Not after Veronica. Never again would he be someone's secret side piece.

It took every ounce of strength not to blow up and say things he would never be able to take back. Instead, he drew in a breath and uttered, "Fine." He turned around and walked toward the door.

"Jason." Libby rushed to catch up with him.

He opened the door and turned to glance at her. "It's fine. Do whatever you want. I need to get to work." He stepped outside, shut the door, and jogged to his SUV.

It wasn't until he'd pulled away from her townhouse and out of sight that he stopped along the side of the road, put the SUV in park, and slammed his hands against the steering wheel. "Fuck."

He couldn't wrap his head around this situation. His head told him to run fast and far. Get away from Libby before she hurt him. She wasn't worth it.

His heart told him she was fucking perfect for him and he needed to calm the fuck down and let her handle this mess in her time. He reminded himself they had only been dating for eleven days. He was putting expectations on her that weren't warranted.

So what if her mother was a bigot? He couldn't expect Libby to tell her parents to go fuck themselves after eleven days with a man, even if the sex *was* off the charts.

Jason needed to shake this off, pull himself together. She said she would handle it. He had to trust that she would. She'd made it clear from their first date that she didn't like people doing things for her. He had to assume this fell under that category. She wanted to fight her own battles. She was a grown woman. She could find a way to make sure Eddie stopped sending gifts. *And, please God, please tell me she will eventually put me first and tell her mom to jump in a lake.*

CHAPTER 19

Libby was stomping furiously when she arrived at her parents' house two hours later. She was mad at them, at Eddie, at Jason, and at herself. She couldn't figure out why Jason was so insistent about her confronting her mom.

Obviously, she would eventually have to face her parents about Jason if things got more serious, but until then, it was not on her shortlist of things to do. That didn't mean she didn't have words for her mom.

She entered the house and went straight for the kitchen where she knew her mother would be prepping for dinner or some shit. The woman loved to cook and was often found in the kitchen, sometimes all day.

Libby knew her father would be at work, but he wasn't the pushy one making her life miserable.

Maria lifted her gaze when she heard Libby enter and smiled. "What a pleasant surprise." She wiped her hands on her apron. "Have you had breakfast? I can put some burritos together for you."

"I've eaten, Mamá. I came to talk to you."

"Okay. Let's sit." She pointed at the table and pulled out a chair.

Libby didn't feel like sitting, but she reluctantly followed, trying to tamp down her aggravation. She decided to dive right in. "Mamá, you have to stop meddling in my life. Why would you invite Eddie to come for dinner without checking with me first?"

Her eyes went wide. "I thought you liked Eddie. I went to a lot of trouble to invite him."

Libby shook her head. "No. You knew I didn't like Eddie. We had one date. We didn't connect. I told you that."

Her mother harrumphed. "I didn't remember you telling me that, and it would seem to me you need to give people more of a chance. He was a charming man last night. I liked him. I don't understand why you're so obstinate." She gasped suddenly. "I hope you're not going to tell me you're not interested in men." Her eyes widened as if that would be a horror worse than death.

Libby groaned. "Jesus, Mamá. What if I wasn't? What if I wanted to date women? Would you disown me?" This was a good test.

Maria rubbed her hands on her apron, flustered. A tear came to her eye. "Is that it? Are you interested in girls, Libby?"

Libby rolled her eyes. "No, Mamá, that's not it. But so what if it was? Truth is, I just don't like Eddie."

"You say that about everyone you date." The woman pouted. *Pouted.*

"And that's my prerogative. You have to stop meddling. I'm not going to settle for someone I'm not in love with. If the sparks aren't there, then there's no reason to keep dating someone."

Her mother shook her head. "That's not true. It's not always love at first sight, Libertad. Sometimes you have to let it grow. Give someone a chance. Eddie is a perfect example.

He's kind, handsome, polite, and he's obviously into you. He comes from good people. His parents have connections. They come from old money. Have you been to his house? It's that brick mansion at the corner of Mason and Deerpark. You know the one?"

Libby gasped. She knew the house, if you could call it that and not a castle. She hadn't realized Eddie owned it.

Her mother kept talking. "You would live a comfortable life with someone like him."

That was enough. She didn't care about Eddie's damn money. Libby slapped her hands on the table, making her mother jump in her seat. "Stop it. Stop trying to fix me up. It's not going to happen with Eddie. It's your fault that he has false hope now, and I have to freaking go talk to him and tell him—*yet again*—that I'm not interested."

"Watch your language, Libertad."

Libby rolled her eyes. *If you even knew how hard it is to substitute freaking for fucking.* She rose from her chair, hands on the table, leaning over. "Stop it. Stop it now. No more dates. No more meddling. Got it?"

Her mother stared at her and then wiped her eyes dramatically. "I'm just trying to help."

"I don't need any help finding a man, Mamá. I'll find one on my own."

Her mother sighed dramatically. "Okay, if you really don't have feelings for Eddie, fine. I'd like you to do me a favor though. One of my neighbors, Josefina Morales, her grandson just moved to Dallas. He doesn't know anyone in town. I already told her you could give him a tour and show him around. Please don't embarrass me and say you won't."

Libby literally growled at her mother.

Her mother sat up straighter. "It wouldn't really be a date. Just being a helpful citizen."

"No." Libby turned and walked out of the house without

looking back. She feared if she'd stayed another second, she would've said things she couldn't take back. It was the first time she'd ever dared to confront her mother.

It felt...good.

Maybe one day she would muster up the confidence to tell her she wasn't marrying a man from Guatemala, too. Because what Libby now realized was that no matter what happened between her and Jason, she was incredibly attracted to him. She was hoping they could continue to build on it.

This was not how she wanted to spend her day. Not even close. She'd intended to go for a run, do some laundry, read a book in her favorite armchair.

Instead, she was on a rampage hunting down people who needed to be set straight.

She'd never been to Eddie's house, nor had she intended to go today. She'd thought she would call him. But now that her mother had told her where he lived, Libby figured it would be easier and faster to just go to the door. It might even send a stronger message.

Granted, Eddie was probably at work. It was the middle of a weekday. But it wouldn't hurt to try. If he happened to be home, she could put an end to this now. If not, she would call him and make him listen.

It took only a few minutes to get to the mansion she'd admired for most of her life. She'd never realized who lived in it. It seemed ridiculous that Eddie owned it. He couldn't have owned it long. He wasn't that old. Mid-twenties. What the hell did he do for a living? He'd never told her. She hadn't cared to ask.

She parked her car in the circular drive and headed for the front door. It was one of those enormous entrances, the double doors wide and tall as if giants lived there.

She rang the bell and waited, wiping her hands on her jeans. She was just about to return to her car when the door finally opened. An older man in his seventies stood there. "Can I help you?"

Libby was taken aback. "I'm looking for Eduardo Lopez. Does he live here?"

"Of course." The man stepped back. "Come in. I'll go tell him you're here. What's your name, miss?"

"Libby. Libertad," she corrected for some odd reason.

He nodded. "Wait right here. I'll be right back." He shuffled off to the left, leaving her to glance around at the foyer. *Jesus.* This place was the wealthiest home she'd ever seen. How was it possible Eddie hadn't mentioned this detail to her?

Several minutes went by before another older man appeared. His eyes were dancing as he reached out a hand. "You must be Libertad Garcia. I've heard so much about you." He was impeccably dressed in pressed dress pants, a white dress shirt, and a black tie. His hair was slicked back, but it was long enough to curl a bit at the back of his neck.

She took his hand, confused beyond measure. "I'm sorry. Who are you?"

"Eduardo Lopez. Eddie's father."

"Oh. I, uh, I'm sorry. I didn't realize..." What the fuck was she supposed to say?

"Come on in. My wife is in the kitchen. She'd love to meet you."

Libby's heart thudded so hard she thought it might jump out of her chest. This could not be happening. It was a nightmare. "I really can't stay, sir. I was looking for Eddie. Is he here?"

"Not right now. He's at the office." He waved his hand, trying to get her to follow him. "But if you're not in a hurry, *Mija,* Elena will have my hide if I tell her you were here and she didn't get to say hello."

"I really can't stay, sir," Libby insisted.

"Who's at the door?" a woman's voice asked from behind.

Great. This disaster was getting worse by the second.

"It's Eddie's girlfriend, Libertad," Eduardo tossed over his shoulder.

"Oh, how delightful." The beaming woman hurried toward Libby. "My God, Eddie was right. You are stunning. Come on in. I'll make tea. Or coffee? Which do you prefer?" Elena was a stunning woman of about fifty. Her hair was stylish and either still black or she dyed it. She wore an expensive skirt and blouse and pumps as if she were heading to the country club at any moment. Maybe she was.

"I'm sorry, ma'am. I can't stay. I was hoping to speak to Eddie. I'll just catch him later."

"Oh, that's too bad." Elena looked seriously defeated, as if Libby's arrival was the most interesting thing that had happened to her in days. "I'll talk to Eddie and make sure he invites you over for dinner soon."

Libby couldn't even respond to that. The hole she was in kept getting deeper. Her world was upside down. "Sorry to bother you," she said as she backed up to the door and then opened it.

"No bother at all, *Mija*," Eduardo insisted. "Please, come again soon."

Libby did nothing but nod and rush down the steps back to her car. She knew the two of them were staring at her from the doorway, so she didn't glance back.

She pulled away, holding her breath, not able to wrap her head around the events of this morning the entire drive home. The moment she was back in her townhouse, she pulled out her phone and shot a text to Eddie.

I went by your house to talk to you. Your parents told me you were at work. I also got your package this morning. I can't accept this. I also thought I made myself clear last night. Nothing is going to happen between us, Eddie. You have to stop sending me gifts.

The fact that the guy lived with his parents didn't escape Libby's attention. What self-respecting grown man lived at home even if they did have a luxurious house with servants? Five minutes later, she received a response.

Oh, good. I'm glad you got my gift. I hope you liked it. I'm sure my parents were delighted to meet you. I don't blame them. I've told them how beautiful and sweet you are. I get that it embarrasses you to receive gifts. You've probably never had a boyfriend who could afford to treat you like you deserve. I can't say I'll stop sending little tokens. I enjoy buying things for you. But I'll give you the space you need to think about us. I know it's overwhelming. I didn't mean for you to figure out how much money I have so soon. It's intimidating. I get that. I'll give you some time. Love, Eddie.

Jesus, this man was infuriating. Libby wanted to throw her phone against the wall. She dropped onto the sofa and leaned back, closing her eyes. She'd never met anyone in her life who wouldn't take no for an answer.

At least he seemed inclined to leave her alone for a while. Hopefully, he would realize she wasn't interested. What else was she supposed to do?

CHAPTER 20

Libby didn't contact Jason all day. She knew he was angry when he left, and she needed to give him space. She kept herself busy doing things around the house until five, and then she drove to his house and waited for him to get home. Was she just as bad as Eddie? Stalking Jason? She shoved the thought from her head. There was no comparison. What she had with Jason was incredible. She cared about him far more than she should have after such a short time.

When she let herself think about it, even his Rambo persona was sexy. The man was possessive. The fact that he'd wanted to hunt Eddie down was attractive, though she wouldn't tell Jason that, nor would she ever agree to let him fight her battles.

Jason pulled into the driveway just after six. His brow was furrowed, but his lips were curled up in a partial smile as he climbed from the SUV and met her gaze. "Hey."

She had climbed out of her car and approached him. When she got close enough, he pulled her into his embrace and held her tight. He nuzzled her neck and kissed behind her ear, making her shiver while at the same time calming her nerves.

When he pulled back and met her gaze, he was smiling broader. "Sorry about this morning."

She shrugged. "My fault. I'm sorry, too. I don't like people to do my dirty work. I've fought my entire life to take care of myself."

"I get that." He brushed a lock of hair from her forehead. "How'd your day go?"

She sighed. "Long story."

"Let's go inside. You can tell me while I make you dinner."

She nearly cried. At least he wasn't still furious. He even held her against his side as they walked to the front door.

Five minutes later, he had her seated on a stool in his kitchen while he took out ingredients to make burgers.

She relayed the morning's events in great detail, including the part about Eddie's parents and his texts. She even showed Jason her phone so he could read the texts.

He leaned over her cell as he read. "Jesus."

"Yeah. That's what I'm thinking."

"You might have to get a restraining order if this guy doesn't back off."

She blew out a breath. "Hopefully it won't come to that."

Jason met her gaze. "Don't freak out on me, but I'd like you to let me put a tracking app on your phone."

"Why?"

"Just in case. Peace of mind. If anything happens to you, at least I'll be able to find you."

"You don't think Eddie would force me to go out with him or something do you?"

Jason shrugged. "I can't begin to know what's in this guy's head. Don't want to find out the hard way. Humor me for a few weeks until this dies down, then you can take the app off if it makes you uncomfortable."

Libby handed Jason her phone. "Okay." It certainly couldn't hurt. It wasn't as if she went to secret places without

Jason. If it made him feel better, it was the easiest way to keep from rocking the boat. Plus, she had to admit, it made her worry less, too.

"Done." He handed it back. "You can easily remove it any time," he reminded her.

"Thank you."

He didn't say another word about her mom or Eddie, and they had a relaxing evening eating and then moving to his room to watch television on his bed.

"When are you going to get living room furniture?" she asked as she snuggled up against his chest.

"I don't think I will. Not if I can count on evenings spent like this." He trailed a hand up her side and cupped her breast, making her arch. So much for watching TV. She'd much rather have this gorgeous man strip off her clothes and remind her how damn good they were together.

CHAPTER 21

Two weeks later…

"Love what you've done to the place," Tank stated sarcastically as he entered Jason's house. He was holding a case of beer so Jason decided against growling at him.

Kraft shouted from the kitchen area across the room. "Hey, man, at least he finally got a kitchen table so he can host poker nights."

Sweets was already in the kitchen also, cutting up whatever delicious dessert he'd brought. "When are you going to get a couch exactly? I mean, the TV looks great hanging on the wall above the fireplace. State of the art. But it's not doing you much good if you can't sit anywhere to watch it," he joked.

The guys were totally right, and Jason had had every intention of finishing the living room last weekend, but since Libby had come into his life, his priorities had shifted significantly. He hadn't had time.

"I don't think his woman cares much about his living room furniture," Kraft taunted.

Jason rolled his eyes as he led Tank toward the kitchen area. "Not one single complaint. You're right."

"How's it going with her, by the way?" Tank asked.

Jason grinned. "Great. Most of the time. If you leave her mother out of the equation. Oh, and the guy she was on a date with when we ran into each other? He's a piece of work, too. Won't take no for an answer."

"Yikes. That's a lot to dissect. Start with her mother." Sweets cringed. "What the hell does her mother have to do with anything?"

Jason sighed as he pulled out a chair and dropped onto it. The rest of the guys sat also. "Apparently she thinks Libby needs to marry a nice man from Guatemala. I don't meet her standards."

Tank winced. "And why does Libby care what her mother thinks?"

Jason shrugged. "I don't know, but I'm close to reaching my limit. It was okay for the first several dates, but I'm losing my patience."

"Are you two exclusive?" Kraft asked.

"Yes. I put my foot down about that the first night we saw each other when I first moved to Dallas."

Tank's eyes went wide. "Wow. I'm not sure I've ever known you to be so territorial about a woman."

Jason took a sip of his beer. "There's always a first for everything. What can I say? We click. I'm falling hard for her. But she's pulling a Veronica."

Kraft groaned. He was the only man at the table who knew about Veronica. She'd been in Jason's life three years ago, long before Jason had met Tank and Sweets.

"Who's Veronica?" Sweets asked.

Kraft glanced at him. "Rich woman who lured Jake into her conniving web, used him, and fucked him over."

"Yep. That about sums it up," Jason agreed.

Kraft continued. "She left scars, and Jason is worried Libby will do the same thing."

"Shit," Tank muttered. "That sucks. Libby's not some rich girl having her cake and eating it too though, is she?"

Jason shrugged. "She's not rich. The rest remains to be seen."

"You need to confront her, man," Kraft nudged. "It's time."

Jason knew his friend was right. Jason had confided in him a few weeks ago, mostly because Kraft knew what had happened with Veronica better than anyone. He wanted to shake this line of questioning though. He spent enough time worrying about Libby and their future. Tonight he wanted to forget. "She has hot friends though if anyone is interested. Three of them. They've all hinted they would love a date with a buff hunk like me. I'm pretty sure they have each asked me if I have any single friends at some point."

Kraft perked up. "What about that blonde, Christa? The one I met at Trent and Destiny's wedding. I call dibs on that one."

Jason laughed. "How did I already know this? And yes, she's single. I'd be happy to set you up if you want. I'll warn you though, she seems pretty innocent."

Kraft rubbed his hands together. "I'd be more than happy to educate her."

Jason rolled his eyes. "I have no doubt."

"Who are the other friends?" Tank asked. "My mom is hounding me for grandkids. I could go for a nice girl."

Sweets groaned. "*Your* mom? Mine's begun to sulk. I'm thirty-nine. You're all just babies compared to me."

"Why don't you find a nice woman and get married then?" Kraft asked.

"You know any? At my age, it's harder. The women I meet are usually carrying a truckload of baggage. I've tried, but I never make it past the first few dates. The last thing I want to do is sneak out of a woman's house before her kids wake up." Sweets shuddered.

"I don't think any of Libby's friends have any baggage like that. They're younger for one thing. You want a sweet girl? I'll set you up with Bex. She's the quietest one."

"That's perfect for you," Kraft teased. "Women can't get a word in edgewise when they're with you."

"Ha-ha." Sweets picked up a chip from the bowl on the table and tossed it at Kraft.

"Okay, matchmaker," Tank said, "who do you have for me?"

"I think Shayla. She looks elegant and sexy. Perfect features."

Tank whistled. "Damn. Do it. I'm in."

Jason glanced around the table at all the expectant faces. "You guys are serious? You want me to set you all up with Libby's friends?"

"Yes." The chorus of agreement was funny.

"You gotta be flexible. These ladies are all flight attendants with crazy schedules."

Everyone nodded.

Kraft stretched his neck to one side and then the other. "See. I'm flexible."

Everyone threw a chip at Kraft.

Jason laughed. At least he was no longer sulking about what to do about Libby. He wasn't sure all her friends would really take him up on his offer, but he could try. They were the ones to originally suggest his matchmaking skills. As long as no one held him responsible for their possible future failures, he didn't care.

Christa was the easiest one. She lived with Libby. He'd

seen her several times. He hoped Kraft wouldn't trounce on her and scare her off in five minutes.

Bex and Shayla had been in the condo one night when he'd picked up Libby. Had they been joking when they insinuated they wanted him to set them up too? Shayla was flirty and funny. She'd done most of the talking. Bex was shy and quiet. She might have agreed with her friends just to not be left out of the banter. She was the biggest wild card.

"Okay. No promises. But I'll ask."

Kraft grabbed the cards and started shuffling. "Are we going to play or plan future dates here?"

"Wait," Tank interrupted. "Hatch didn't tell us about this guy Libby was dating. What's up with that?"

Jason groaned. "Name's Eddie. They had the one date. One. And the man won't leave her alone. He sent her roses for nearly two weeks and then he sent her a dress that in my opinion doesn't have enough material to leave the house in. If she were mine—and hell, in my mind, she is—I'd never share that much of her skin with other people."

The guys laughed and Kraft spoke again. "That's kinda creepy. Have you confronted him?"

"No. Libby doesn't like people fighting her battles. I'm trying to keep my mouth shut and let her handle it. For now. He keeps texting her every three or four days. And she keeps telling him there isn't a chance in hell she'll go out with him again. I've read the texts. She's doing her best."

"What if things escalate?" Sweets asked.

"Then I'll be grateful I have three friends who will gladly bring the shovel, bury the body, and not ask questions." He smiled. He was kidding of course. Sort of. But he did know he could count on his friends if he needed to confront Eddie.

He couldn't really blame Libby. She tried. The guy was apparently dense or stupid. He was also rich. Jason had looked him up, done some digging online. His family had money.

Jason wasn't sure where it all came from. They owned a business, but whatever they actually did eluded Jason.

He had his suspicions the company wasn't on the up-and-up, but he hadn't told Libby. He didn't want to scare her. He was nervous enough for both of them. But he was paying close attention. If anything began to smell rotten, he would not hesitate to hunt this Eddie guy down and put an end to his freaky obsession.

CHAPTER 22

"You're quiet today," Libby said as she flopped down on a beige couch in the furniture store. "Everything okay?"

Jason nodded. "Yep. Just fine." He pointed at the sofa. "You think I should go with something neutral like this or something with a splash of color?" He knew nothing about what might be fashionable as it concerned living room furniture, nor did he care, but he didn't want to talk about why he was growing impatient right now either.

"Beige for the couch. Colors for the throw pillows. That way when you get tired of a color scheme, all you have to do is replace the pillows." She patted the cushion next to her. "What matters is how it feels. You're going to spend a lot of time sitting on this furniture. It has to be comfortable."

He lowered onto the cushion next to her and leaned back. It felt like he was sitting on a couch. *What the hell is she talking about?*

"What do you think?" she asked.

"It's fine."

"Fine? That's not really what you should be going for here. Let's try another one."

When she started to stand, he grabbed her hand and pulled her back down next to him. "I don't really care about the fucking couch. Gotta be honest."

She sighed. "I can see that. You want to tell me what's bothering you then?" She bit her bottom lip.

He glanced around. He hadn't meant to have this serious discussion right here in the store. "Let's get out of here. I'm not in the mood to buy a couch today."

"Okay," she whispered, squeezing his hand.

Jason pulled her to standing and led her from the store. He never should have let her talk him into furniture shopping today. As soon as they were back in his SUV, he turned to face her. "I want to meet your parents."

She winced before glancing away.

The more he hounded her, the more important this became to him because the longer she put him off, the less faith he had that she ever intended to share him with her family. That got way the fuck under his skin.

"Jason…" she groaned. "I'm not ready for that. You can't begin to understand what you're asking from me."

He stared at her. "I know exactly what I'm asking from you. I'm asking you to tell your parents you have a boyfriend. If you can't do that, I think we should stop seeing each other."

She gasped. "You're serious?"

"Yes." He hadn't meant to say that. It hadn't been part of his planned speech, but the words came out, and he wouldn't take them back. He meant every word.

Libby twisted her fingers together in her lap, not meeting his gaze.

He could guess why she was waffling. He just couldn't tolerate it anymore. "I know we've only been seeing each other for about a month, but we've spent a lot of time together. We have a connection. I know you feel it too. I'm a smart guy. I get that you're hesitating because you don't want to upset your entire family dynamic unnecessarily. You don't want to say anything to them until you feel confident this thing with us is solid."

She winced. "You make me sound very shallow."

He held her gaze. "I'm just trying to make you understand my feelings. I'm telling you this *is* solid for me. As solid as any relationship I've ever been in. I'm not saying I can guarantee forever because it's too soon for that. What I am saying is that I'm not willing to even find out if you don't put me as a higher priority. And, more importantly, your reluctance to tell your parents about me is contributing to the fact that Eddie is still contacting you. The two things are tied together. Your parents are apparently friends with Eddie's. If you tell them you have a boyfriend, it'll get back to Eddie. You have to realize it's maddening to me that fucking guy keeps texting you, and you never tell him you're with someone else."

He waited. He didn't really have anything else to say about this subject. He was right about this. He was also totally into this woman. Every time they were together, their connection was more and more obvious. They had a great time when they went out, and an even better time when they returned to his place and he dominated her in the bedroom. He'd added floggers and even a crop to their play. Libby reacted to everything he introduced her to with louder moaning and stronger orgasms.

Chemistry was not their problem. Not in or out of bed. But he'd had it with her reluctance to share him with her family. He'd been down this road before and it had ended very badly.

"Okay," she finally murmured. She lifted her gaze to his. "I have to go to my parents' house for dinner Saturday night. I'll tell them then."

He sat up taller. "You will?"

"Yes. You're right. It's time for me to face them." She chewed on her bottom lip.

"And what if they react badly?" he asked. He couldn't grasp anyone's parents shunning them for who they chose as a partner, but this was apparently a possibility.

She sighed. "I don't know."

"Well, you need to decide what's more important to you. If you want to go back to dating only men your mother chooses for you, go ahead. I'll step out of the picture and let you go on with your life. If you can't face them with the truth, it tells me everything I need to know—that I'm not that important to you."

She flinched and lifted her gaze to his again. "Jason, that's not true. You're very important to me. But you can't understand how disastrous this could be. Rocking the boat with my mom is risky. I've always known that. When I do what she wants, or at least feign to do so, there is peace in the family. I wouldn't put it past her to kick me out of the house and change the locks if I defy her."

He nodded. "I understand. You've made that clear. But I'm done lying. So what if she kicks you out of the house? You don't live there. You're a grown woman with your own place. If you're going to be with me, we're going to stop sneaking around. You choose."

She drew in a breath. "Okay. I said I would. I will. Saturday night."

"You want me to go with you?"

"No." She shook her head. "I'll do it. It's better if I do it alone."

He watched her face, knowing she was totally uncomfortable with his ultimatum. He needed to think of himself, however. He knew she was into him. She spent every night when she wasn't working with him, either out or at his place. Every day that he spent with her was better than the last.

He wanted her. He wanted *more*.

Could she put him first? If not, they had nothing. He wouldn't continue sneaking around with the woman he was falling in love with. Not again. Never again. He'd let this go on too far already.

CHAPTER 23

Libby was nervous when she arrived at her parents' house Saturday night. She'd gone back and forth in her mind, wondering if she should have let Jason come with her. She knew she'd hurt him by denying him the option.

The truth was, she expected this to go very badly. She didn't want him to see how ridiculously insensitive her mother could be. It was embarrassing. She feared if she brought Jason to her parents' home, they might ignore him entirely as if he didn't exist. And that was the best-case scenario. She didn't want to have to worry about Jason's feelings while she was pleading her case.

The last few weeks had been stressful with her mother. Libby hadn't been to the house a single time, but her mother had called every few days. It didn't do any good to ignore her. She would just call back until Libby answered.

Every conversation went the same. Maria continued to harp about Eddie out of one side of her mouth while also hounding Libby to entertain her neighbor's grandson, and Libby continued to put her off with excuses about needing to work and being too busy.

It was time. If Libby didn't confront her mother now, she would lose the best thing to ever happen to her.

Jason had been patient with her long enough. She knew that. He'd made it clear early on in their relationship that he didn't like the secrets, but he'd given her space. Three weeks of amazing dates and even better sex.

She had never dated a man as perfect as him. She'd never dreamed such a man even existed for her. Jason was not only amazing company outside the bedroom, but he blew the doors off when it came to sex.

Libby closed her eyes and took a deep breath, trying to calm her heart. Thoughts of being blindfolded and bound to Jason's bed filled her mind. He'd stretched her out on her stomach last weekend, wrists and ankles pulled tight to the four corners of his bed. After demonstrating how damn good a flogger felt, he'd fucked her in that position so hard she'd come without direct contact to her clit.

Taking a deep breath for fortification, Libby shook the thoughts from her head and focused on what needed to be done here. She wouldn't give up Jason to appease her mother. Not a chance. That was asking too much. Now she just needed to find a way to explain herself and pray her mother didn't decide to kick her out of the family.

Libby dragged herself to the front door. The moment she opened it, the hairs on the back of her neck stood up. Several people were in the living room. Not just her parents. *Why am I not surprised to find a man near my age among them?*

Libby gritted her teeth as her mother rushed forward to hug her. "Finally! I was beginning to think you wouldn't show up."

Libby let her mother hug her but barely returned the affection. She was already livid. Warning bells were ringing loudly in her head.

And sure enough, her mother spun around and motioned for

the man speaking to her father to join them. "Libby, this is Javier. I told you about him. He's new in town. I thought you could take him to that Mexican restaurant on 3rd street that you love. Maybe drive around a bit afterward and give him the lay of the land."

Libby's face heated. She was going to kill her mother. The woman was high-handed and frequently overstepped, but this was beyond the pale. She had totally cornered Libby.

Javier looked chagrined. At least he wasn't as cocky as some of the other men her mother set her up with. "We don't have to do that. It's not like I can't figure out my way around Dallas without help," he joked.

Maria shook her head and turned toward Libby. "It's no bother at all. Is it, Libertad?"

For the first time in Libby's life, she truly wanted to scream at her mother and stomp out of the house. However, there were other people in the room. Not just her father, but an older couple Libby recognized as neighbors from two doors down. Undoubtedly they were Javier's grandparents.

"You two go. Have fun. You don't need to hang around here with the rest of us." Maria practically shoved them toward the door.

Libby hadn't even had a chance to say hello to her father. When she glanced his direction, he gave her a little wave, his expression indicating he thought this matchup was a great idea.

Before Libby could protest at all, she found herself on the porch with Javier.

Javier tucked the tips of his fingers into his jeans. He chuckled nervously. "You knew nothing about this, did you?"

"No." She lifted her gaze to him. This was not his fault. "Sorry. My mom…"

"Yeah, I get that. My grandmother is the same way. Always trying to match me up with someone. Look, we don't have to go out. We could just leave and go our separate ways. None of them will ever know. We can tell them later we didn't feel the connection."

Libby sighed. Javier was a nice guy. He didn't deserve this shitshow. This was not his fault, and he seemed like a good guy. She also knew exactly the sort of hell he might have to face from his grandparents if they didn't at least go to dinner, and she didn't want to put that on him.

She took a deep breath and glanced at the door. "We're here now. We have to eat. Might as well appease them and report back. As friends," she added.

Javier offered a wan smile. "I don't mind if you don't."

Yeah. He'd definitely catch hell, but he was trying to spare her. Libby led him to her car. "I'll drive."

Her hands were shaking as she entered the Honda and started the engine. She didn't say a word during the three-minute drive to the neighborhood restaurant.

When they were seated, she ordered iced tea and finally met Javier's gaze.

He ordered a beer. "Do you have a boyfriend?"

"Yes." This was the first time she'd said that out loud to anyone who knew her mother. "I haven't told my mother. She wouldn't approve."

He nodded. "I get that. My own parents aren't as particular about who I date, but I've come to realize my grandparents are still old school. I think they're hoping that now that I'm here staying with them for a while they'll be able to find me a nice woman they approve of."

Libby smiled. *This isn't so bad.* At least Javier understood and was on the same page. "It's ridiculous, and I hate that I'm scared to tell my parents the truth."

Javier sighed. "I hear ya. One year, about five years ago, I had a serious girlfriend who was Asian. When my parents told my grandparents, you'd think they had announced that I was in love with a blue alien from another planet."

Libby laughed. "That's what I'm worried about. I dated a Mexican once and didn't even tell them because I knew they would lose their shit."

Javier chuckled. "Gasp. How could you?" he joked.

Libby relaxed. "What happened with your girlfriend?"

He winced. "I didn't bring her to Dallas with me for Christmas, and she broke up with me. She was totally right. I should have stayed home with her or faced my grandparents, but I was weak and didn't feel like rocking the boat."

Libby cringed. "Yeah, the clock is ticking with Jason, too. In fact, I told him I was going to face my parents tonight. I came to the house ready to lay it all out."

"And then you found a houseful of people." He blew out a breath. "I'm so sorry."

"Not your fault."

"You seem like a very nice woman. Jason is lucky to have you. For what it's worth, I think you should confront your parents and stand by your man. After all, your future is not with your mom and dad. You need to spend it with someone you love. Don't make the mistake I made and let it go on much longer."

"You're right." She sat up straighter and smiled. "Thanks for the pep talk. I needed a kick in the pants."

CHAPTER 24

Jason spent most of Saturday pacing his empty living room, worrying about Libby and her conversation with her parents. He knew she was going to their house for dinner at six, and he kept glancing at the clock, wondering when she might call him and stressing over the thought of her facing them alone.

She didn't have to do that. He would have gone with her. No matter what, he should be at her side. After all, it was on his insistence that she was even confronting them in the first place.

At five-thirty, he decided to join her. She hadn't invited him, but he figured her decision to go alone was out of embarrassment. He could handle her parents. No matter what happened, he wanted to be by Libby's side, not sitting at home waiting like a wuss.

What kind of boyfriend would let his girlfriend face a challenge on her own? It suddenly seemed ridiculous, so he grabbed his keys from the kitchen counter and rushed out the door. He figured he could still catch her before she left her condo and drive her to her parents himself.

Instead, he hit every red light and was disappointed to see

her car wasn't out in front of her condo. He jogged to the door anyway, hoping Christa would be home.

Christa opened the door, her expression confused. "Libby isn't here."

"I know. She's having dinner with her parents. I should have gone with her. Do you have their address?"

Christa's mouth fell open and then she closed it. "You think that's a good idea? I've met her parents. They're not very..."

He nodded. "I know. I'm aware. But I'm the one who insisted she tell them about me. I should have gone with her."

Christa licked her lips. "I agree, and that's incredibly nice of you. I'll go grab the address. Come on in."

She spun around and headed for the kitchen area as Jason stepped inside.

A minute later she returned, holding out a piece of paper. "For what it's worth, I think you're the best thing that's ever happened to Libby. She's head over heels for you." She handed him the address. "If you have any brothers or friends who are as doting as you are, give them my number." Her pale cheeks turned red and she glanced away after she spoke, embarrassed.

"I do in fact. Not brothers, but friends. If you don't mind, I'll give my friend Mack your number."

She pursed her lips and nodded, her face turning redder. Finally, she smiled at him. "Go. Hunt down Libby and show her how much you care."

"Thank you." He turned and rushed back to his SUV at a jog.

His hands were shaking as he fumbled with the door and then headed toward the address on the paper. He could have used the GPS tracker on her phone to locate her, but she'd be moving right now. He didn't want to wait until she arrived to leave her condo.

160

When he pulled up to the house ten minutes later, he didn't see Libby's car. He checked the house number again and then decided to go to the door. The worst thing that could happen was he would find out he was at the wrong place.

He could hear several voices inside when he knocked on the door, and a few moments later a woman who looked exactly like an older version of Libby answered. "Can I help you?" she asked curtly.

"Are you Mrs. Garcia? Libby's mom?"

She straightened her shoulders, rising to her full height of barely five feet in the same way he'd seen Libby do many times. "I am. Who are you?"

"I'm…a friend of Libby's. I thought she was here. Is she not?"

Maria Garcia shook her head, a smile forming on her lips. "No. She's on a date. They went to Don Juan's, the Mexican restaurant a few blocks south of here."

Jason stared at Maria for several seconds. "A date?"

"Yes, of course. Javier is a lovely man. Just moved here. She took him to dinner and then she's going to show him around the area. I wouldn't expect them back until late." She looked so proud of herself for divulging her daughter's whereabouts. In great detail.

Maybe she sensed that Jason was interested in her daughter and thought she could steer him away with her information.

Maybe she was right.

Jason nodded slowly, dumbfounded. "Thank you." He turned around and headed back toward his SUV, reminding himself it was possible Mrs. Garcia had exaggerated the story.

Jason settled in his seat, slowly pulled his seatbelt on, and then stared out the windshield. Was it possible Libby was seriously on a date with some guy named Javier? Had she been dating her mother's preferential men all this time on the side?

He shook that last part out of his head. There was no way Libby was courting multiple men. She didn't have time. She was with Jason nearly every night she wasn't working. Unless she was also lying about even having a job as a flight attendant, she couldn't be seeing other people.

But what about tonight? Who the hell is Javier?

There was only one way to find out.

Jason opened his phone and used the app to locate Libby. Sure enough, Libby was indeed at Don Juan's. Jason started the engine, and pulled away from the house. It took less than three minutes to reach the restaurant, and Jason immediately spotted Libby's Honda in the parking lot. At least that part was true. She was undoubtedly eating at Don Juan's.

Jason's heart pounded as he stepped down from his car and headed for the entrance. The place was crowded. Not surprising. As he pushed through the front door, he reminded himself to calm down. He scanned the restaurant and immediately found her.

Libby. His Libby. The woman he'd fallen in love with in less than a month. The woman who was everything he'd ever wanted in a partner. The spunky woman who managed everything on her own to prove she could do anything she set her mind to. The one who turned that power over to him as soon as he shut the bedroom door.

She looked as gorgeous as ever, and she was smiling genuinely at the man across from her.

For a minute, Jason simply stood there staring, unsure how the hell he wanted to proceed.

And then Libby's face turned his way. The moment she spotted him, her expression fell and she jumped to her feet.

Jason glanced from her shocked expression to her date and back. He didn't need an explanation. He could see perfectly well with his own eyes that indeed Libby had gone out with another man while she was supposed to be at her parents' house telling them she had a boyfriend.

He turned around and pushed the door open, leaving the restaurant. He took long, fast strides to cross the parking lot, his heart thumping with fury.

"*Jason*," Libby yelled from behind him.

He knew he had several yards on her, so he picked up the pace and made it to his car before she caught up with him. She must have been running.

"It's not what you think," she began.

He glared at her and then yanked his car door open and climbed in. "Really? Because it looks to me like instead of telling your parents you have a serious boyfriend, you're out on a date with another man, which confirms what your mom told me."

Her eyes went wide. "You spoke to my mom?"

"Don't look so shocked, Libby." He grabbed the door.

"You're just going to leave? Without letting me explain?" She took a step back.

"What the hell is there to explain, Libby? Clearly, I'm just your dirty little secret. I don't think you have any intention of ever telling your parents about me." He was furious and hurt and pissed-off with himself for letting things go this far. He'd seen the signs all along. *Why did I let her string me along all this time?*

Libby gasped. "Jason."

"How long did you plan to carry on this farce? Did you think you could use me for good sex while continuing to search for a suitable man to marry?"

She gasped.

He gripped the door handle. "I'm done, Libby. I'm not your plaything. Been there. Done that. Won't do it again." He tipped his head back and gave a sardonic laugh. "Guess I already did though, didn't I? I let you string me along for a month. At least I got wiser sooner this time. Enjoy your life, Libby. Find someone else to fuck on the side while you marry a boring man who pleases your mom. It's not going to be me."

Jason shook with fury as he shut the door, started the engine, and pulled away. He didn't give a shit that she was standing in the parking lot still talking. His pride was hurt in a big way, and he was far too angry to continue this conversation.

Instead of going home, Jason decided he needed a drink. More than one. He turned in the direction of a local bar where he sometimes met up with the guys.

Just as he was pulling in, his phone rang. He glanced at it, determined to ignore Libby entirely. The incoming call was from Kraft. Jason stared at it a moment and then took the call. "I'm kinda busy right now, Kraft. Do you need me for anything important?"

Kraft's breath hitched. "You okay? You sound incredibly pissed."

"I'm way the fuck past pissed. I'm about to get drunk at The Draft."

"Shit. I'll be there in ten." Kraft hung up.

Jason jerked his car door open. He wasn't sure he wanted company while he nursed his anger, but if anyone was going to join him, he would want it to be Kraft. Hell, he hadn't even asked the man why he was calling in the first place. He was furious with Libby and on top of that, a shitty friend.

After grabbing two beers from the bar—both intended for himself—Jason slumped into a booth and downed the first beer in one long drink. It took the edge off just enough that when Kraft walked in, Jason's heart wasn't beating quite as fast.

Kraft immediately slid into the booth across from him and

got the waitresses attention, ordering two more beers. "What happened?"

"I'm an idiot. That's what happened. Apparently, I didn't learn a damn thing from Veronica."

Kraft winced. "Libby? Surely you don't mean to tell me that Libby is anything like Veronica."

Jason ran a hand through his hair and then took another swig. "Possibly worse."

"What did she do?"

"She has no spine. Not only did she not tell her parents about us still, but she's fucking dating other men."

Kraft's eyes widened. "Are you sure? That doesn't sound like Libby at all."

Jason gave a sardonic laugh. "Oh, trust me. I'm sure. I saw her. I went to the restaurant where she was currently out with her latest blind date, courtesy of her mother, and saw her with my own fucking eyes. She was even smiling at the guy as if he was the best date she'd been on in months."

Kraft winced. "What did she say?"

"I didn't give her a chance to talk. I was too angry. And besides, what the hell was she going to say? There was nothing to explain. I caught her with another man. Period." Jason picked at the label on his beer, tearing it into strips until a pile of curled soaked paper piled up in front of him.

Kraft looked skeptical, but he didn't argue the point further.

"I had a chat with her roommate earlier this evening though. She said she would go out with you. If you want her number, get it from Libby. I'm done with women."

Kraft set his elbows on the table. "Christa? The blonde?"

"Yep."

"Okay, let's return to that subject another time. For now, let's discuss what you're going to do about Libby. I know this isn't casual for you. You're totally into her. You've been a different person since you started dating her. She's important. Dare I say more important than Veronica ever was."

Jason blew out a breath. Kraft was right. He was so screwed.

Kraft continued, his voice calmer. "I think you need to talk to her. Let her tell her side. At least do that before you toss her into the lake."

Jason groaned as he tipped his head back. The second beer was doing its job. He might feel like shit tomorrow, but he didn't care right now.

"Why did you come here?" Kraft asked.

"So she couldn't find me."

"That's what I figured, which means you think she will try to find you, which tells you she has something to say. You're hiding."

Jason laughed out loud, manically. "Yep. That's me. Hiding. It's in both our best interests that I remain in hiding for tonight. If I don't, I'll end up saying things I can't take back."

Kraft smiled. "See? If you're also worried that you might stick your foot in your mouth, that tells me you care."

Jason downed the rest of his beer and grabbed Kraft's second one. "For now, I just want to get drunk. It doesn't matter if I care or not. I'm done with conniving women who only keep me around as some kind of side toy."

CHAPTER 25

Libby was a mess by the time she rushed into her condo a few hours later.

Christa was on the couch watching TV. She jumped up when Libby entered. "Oh my God. What happened?"

Libby knew she looked awful. She'd been crying. Her face was streaked in tears. Her eyes had to be puffy and red. She dropped onto the sofa next to Christa and started crying yet again. "I fucked up."

"Oh shit. Did Jason find you? He came here looking for you. Said he wanted to go to your parents with you. I gave him their address. I'm so sorry if I overstepped." Christa's voice wobbled.

Libby shook her head and wiped at her tears. "Not your fault. This is on me. He could have tracked me with the GPS anyway. He asked me to tell my parents about us repeatedly. I was weak and chicken, so I didn't do it. I was going to tonight. I meant to. But then my mother sabotaged my evening with another one of her blind dates."

"Oh no." Christa winced.

"Yeah. He must have gone to my parents' house first. I bet

my mother was more than happy to tell him in her flourishing way that I was on a date and where I was." Libby grabbed a pile of tissues from the end table and wiped her eyes.

"Why would you go out with someone else even if you were blindsided?" Christa cautiously asked.

Libby groaned. "It's complicated. Javier was in the same boat as me. We decided to commiserate together and share our stories. It was harmless." Libby sat up straighter. "And I'm furious with Jason for not even letting me explain. He just took off. I ran after him, but he wouldn't listen."

Christa cringed. "Can you blame him?"

Libby shook her head. "No. But I'm still angry. He didn't trust me."

"What happened next? Why are you here instead of groveling?"

"Because I couldn't find him. He didn't go home. I waited for a while outside his house, but he never showed up."

"He can't stay gone forever," Christa pointed out tentatively. "It's his home. He probably needed to cool down somewhere before he spoke to you."

"Yeah, well, I'm exhausted and pretty angry with myself now, so he can have all the time he wants to cool down. I'm going to bed." Libby shoved off the couch and stood. She leaned down and hugged Christa. "Thanks for listening. I'm sorry to dump on you."

Christa smiled. "Any time. You know that. We're friends."

Libby swiped at another tear. "I know, but...well, thank you." She turned and shuffled toward the stairs. This was not how she'd imagined her evening ending. Not by a long shot. She'd spent the day imagining arguing with her parents and possibly being kicked out of her childhood home by an irrational mother. In that scenario, she'd pictured ending up in Jason's bed at the end of the night, probably crying on his shoulder until he calmed her down.

Libby stripped out of her clothes and pulled on an old T-shirt before turning off the lights and climbing into bed. She curled onto her side and let another wave of tears fall. She was mad at herself for not being more assertive with her mother. She was mad at her mother for being so intolerant and putting Libby in this position in the first place. She was also mad at Jason for being so stubborn that he wouldn't listen to reason.

Why does everything have to be so damn complicated?

Something he'd said came rushing back into her mind. *Been there. Done that. Won't do it again.* She wondered what the hell he'd been referring to. It was such a specific thing to say. And it made no sense.

Libby groaned as she rolled onto her back and remembered everything that had transpired last night. She tossed her forearm over her eyes to block the light coming in from the open blinds that she hadn't bothered to shut the night before.

After a few deep breaths, she reached for her phone on the nightstand and found no new texts or calls.

Shit. She couldn't decide if the ball was in her court or his right now. After all, he was the one who stormed off and sped away from her while she was trying to explain. Then again, she was the one who had no spine, which caused him to find her in a compromising position in the first place.

She considered sending him a text and then spent at least fifteen minutes typing and retyping words before finally hitting send.

Can we talk? Please call me.

She didn't expect an immediate response. After all, it was

early in the morning. He was probably out late and sleeping in. However, an hour later after she'd showered and dressed and had some coffee, she switched from thinking it was too early to thinking he was ignoring her text.

An hour after that, she was pissed. *Fuck him.* If he didn't want to listen to reason, fine. She didn't need that shit in her life.

Two hours after that, she decided to go to the grocery store and run a few errands. There was no food in the condo. She still hadn't eaten yet today, and her stomach was rumbling, but the thought of chewing and swallowing was more than she could handle.

Christa was in the kitchen grabbing a soda from the fridge when Libby returned with an armload of grocery bags. "Hey," Christa said softly. "You okay? Did you find Jason?"

Libby shook her head. "Didn't even try."

Christa's eyes went wide. "Why not?"

"I sent him a text first thing this morning asking him if we could talk. He didn't respond. I get that I'm partly to blame for this fiasco, but if the man won't even let me explain myself, I'm not going to go over there begging and groveling."

Christa cleared her throat. "Maybe you should?" she hedged.

Libby put the carton of milk in the fridge and turned around. "Nope. Not going to happen. I've worked my entire life to be strong and independent. I'm not going to let anyone make me feel like I'm not worth listening to."

"When do you work next?" Christa asked as she unloaded one of the bags.

"Monday afternoon."

Christa yanked the bag Libby was holding out of her hands. "Go."

"Go where? What are you talking about?"

Christa pointed to the door. "Go find him. Make this right.

Do it now. Don't spend the next day and a half moping around kicking yourself and him. Face him. Talk to him."

Libby rolled her eyes. "Give me one good reason why I should be the one to confront him when he drove away from me last night and didn't answer my text this morning."

"Because you're in love with him."

Libby sucked in a breath, blinking at her friend.

Christa narrowed her gaze. "Deny it."

"You're right."

"Go." She pointed toward the door again.

Libby hesitated a few more seconds and then leaned in to hug Christa. "Thank you again." She grabbed her keys and rushed back out the door.

CHAPTER 26

Jason was sitting on his back deck, nursing his second cup of coffee when movement to the side of his house caught his eye. He jerked his gaze to find Libby entering his backyard through the gate.

His breath hitched as he watched her body sway with every slow step in his direction. He didn't say a word, but he was unnerved to realize that even though he was still nursing a solid mad, he was attracted to her.

She looked chagrined. After taking the two steps up to his deck and sitting on the side of the second lounge chair facing him, she drew in a breath. "You didn't answer the door but your car was in the driveway, so I thought maybe..." She glanced down at her lap, fisting her hands together.

He furrowed his brow, reminding himself that she'd treated him badly and nothing she could say would make up for the way she'd behaved. He'd gone over everything that happened last night several times this morning, and in no scenario did she redeem herself.

She changed the subject. "You didn't answer my text."

He lifted one brow higher. Part of him didn't feel the desire to even respond to her. "I wasn't up when you sent it."

"You're up now."

"And I'm still too angry to talk to you." That much was true, though at this point he'd decided it would never subside. "Besides, I don't have anything to say."

She took a deep breath and sat up straighter. "Okay, well, maybe I could talk, and you could just listen."

He shrugged as if he didn't care one way or another.

"When I got to my parents' last night, I had a whole speech ready. I promise. And then I opened the front door and there were several people in the living room. My mother had been hounding me to meet her neighbors' grandson. I'd put her off every time, telling her I had to work or that I was too busy."

Jason knew all this. Or he could piece it together.

"She stepped way over the line this time. Putting me in an awkward position."

Jason groaned and dramatically rolled his head back to stare at the sky. She thought *she* was in an awkward position? What about him?

"I know. I know. I should have told the entire room that I couldn't go out with Javier because I had a boyfriend. I should have confronted my mother in front of her neighbors and stood up for myself once and for all. It just all happened so fast. In seconds, she had introduced me to Javier and shoved us out the front door telling Javier I would take him to dinner and show him around town."

Jason lowered his head to shoot her with a glare.

Libby released her hands to pinch the bridge of her nose. "As soon as the door closed, I realized Javier was actually very understanding. He could sense my discomfort. He immediately guessed that I had a boyfriend. And, on top of everything else, it turned out we had a lot in common. His grandparents treat him the same way my parents treat me—as if no person who isn't Guatemalan will ever be good enough."

Jason couldn't hold back his sarcastic thoughts another moment. "Well, isn't that just perfect. You two will be so happy together. I wish you all the best."

Libby shook her head. "No. That's not what I'm saying. I'm trying to tell you that it was innocent. I talked to Javier about you and he spoke to me about his previous girlfriend whom he lost when he didn't put her first. He made me understand that I have to put you first if I really care about you or I'll regret it for the rest of my life."

Jason swung around to sit on the side of his lounge chair facing her. His blood was boiling. "You needed to go out with another guy to realize you *care* about me?"

Her bottom lip was trembling and she glanced down at her lap again. "No. I didn't. But I was blindsided, Jason. I didn't want to cause a scene in front of Javier's grandparents. We chose to appease them and walk away. I get that you don't understand how I'm feeling or how much pressure I'm under, but I'm trying."

Jason jumped to his feet and started pacing. "You don't have the first clue what I understand, Libby. I may not have a college degree like you, but I'm not stupid. I'm just some dirty little secret you keep on the side with no intention of ever telling anyone about me. Some dumb guy from Iowa who grew up on a farm and never went to college. Sure, the sex is great, but that's about it. Why bother to upset your family when you don't intend to keep me around when the sex gets boring anyway?"

Libby jerked her head in his direction. "What the hell are you talking about? Dirty little secret? You're not any such thing. I brag about you to all my friends so often they're growing tired of me. I didn't even know you were from Iowa. You've never talked about your childhood. I didn't know you don't have a college degree either. Nor do I care. Why the hell would that matter to me? When have I ever once insinuated I thought I was better than you?"

Jason stopped pacing when he realized he wasn't speaking to Veronica. He was speaking to Libby. Somehow during the last twelve hours, he'd converged the two of them into one person. He ran a hand through his hair and came back to sit facing her, several inches separating them. Silence reigned for several moments before he finally took a deep breath and let it out. "I had a girlfriend three years ago. Her name was Veronica."

Libby froze, not saying a word.

Jason braced himself to share this story, a tale he'd kept buried deep inside most of the time, not wanting to bring it out or confront it. "I met her at a bar when I was on leave during the holidays. She seemed sweet and kind and fun, so we started dating."

Libby reached out as if to touch Jason's thigh but then pulled her hand back and gripped her knees.

"She was rich. Her family owned a department store. Weeks went by and she never once suggested introducing me to her parents or her siblings. Every time I mentioned it, she put me off, saying she didn't want to waste our time together sharing me with other people."

Libby sucked in a sharp breath but didn't interrupt him.

He continued, glancing at her fleetingly. "It took me months to realize all I was to her was arm candy. She liked to go out with me because she was attracted to me and she thought we made a cute couple. The sex was good, too." He at least had the decency to lower his voice as he said that last part.

"What happened?" Libby whispered.

"I woke up one morning and wandered into my kitchen to find her on the phone. Her back was to me, and she didn't hear me approaching. She was talking to her fiancé. Her *real* boyfriend. The man she intended to marry in six months. The one who was good enough for her and had her family's approval."

Libby pursed her lips. She looked close to tears.

Jason kept talking. He needed to finish. "When she hung up and spun around, finding me leaning against the table with my arms crossed, she stuttered and then gave me this lame pile of excuses about how much more fun I was and how her regular life was not her own. She pleaded with me to not only continue seeing her but to do so even after the wedding. Totally in secret."

"Jesus, Jason. I'm so sorry. Why didn't you ever tell me all of this?"

He swiped a palm down his face. "Because it's humiliating and I try not to think about it."

"Except you *did* think about it…*all* the time. You worried that what we have would end the same way."

"Yes." She was right.

"I'm not Veronica, Jason. I don't have another man I'm secretly seeing on the side. Nothing about you embarrasses me. You're amazing. You're smart and hard-working and sexy as hell and you rock my world in the bedroom. I don't give a single shit about how much education you have. Hell, my degree is downright embarrassing. Nearly everyone I tell gets a laugh at my expense. Who works their ass off to get a liberal arts degree and then goes to flight attendant school?"

Jason shook his head. "Someone who's driven and dedicated and determined to prove to the world that she may be petite on the outside, but she is not to be fucked with on the inside." He gave her a wan smile. "You're totally put-together. You have everything. Strength I envy. You can do anything you set your mind to. And that's great. It's attractive. It's what draws me to you. I used to think I was some dumb kid from Iowa who didn't have the grades or the money for college, so I joined the Army. They taught me I was worth something, even without coming from money or earning a fancy degree. They taught me to have pride in myself. So I won't be some dirty little secret for a woman ever again. If you can't scream from the roof that I'm your man, I'm done."

Libby lurched forward and grabbed his hands, squeezing them against his thighs. "You're absolutely right. I've fucked this up. I should have had the balls to tell my parents about you from the moment we met. I've been a coward. Hell, I should have stood up to my mother years ago even before I met you. I never should have let her dictate who I date."

He stared at her. After all, this is what he'd been telling her all along.

She drew in a breath. "But back to you. You don't need a ton of money or a fucking degree to prove anything to anyone. It's just a piece of paper. You're intelligent and hard-working. You have an amazing job that's way the hell over my head. You're worth ten thousand other men. A stronger woman than me would have dragged you home the night we met and told her parents how important you were, to hell with their reactions."

He rolled his eyes as he flipped his hands over and grasped hers.

"I'm in love with you, Jason. You're everything to me. Nothing matters as much as you. Yes, it scares the hell out of me to tell my parents because I'm afraid they will literally cut me out of their lives. That doesn't mean I shouldn't do it, nor does it mean I won't. It just means I'm scared. That's a horrible excuse for my behavior. I've been weak, and it wasn't fair to you. And I'm so, so sorry."

He released her hands and reached out to grab her around the waist and haul her onto his lap. He held her tightly, his face buried in her hair as he inhaled her scent and tried to calm his racing heart.

She wrapped her arms around him and stroked his back. "I'm so sorry, Jason," she repeated against his chest. Finally, she tipped her head back and met his gaze. "I'm in love with you, and I swear there's no other man I care about. There never will be."

He set his forehead against hers and closed his eyes, trying to assure himself this was real.

"As for the sex, you're wrong about that too. It will never get boring between us. Every time we're together it gets better. Every time you dominate me, my heart races faster than the last time. My body burns for you."

He smiled at her and then smashed his lips to hers as he threaded his fingers in her hair at the back of her head and angled her just where he wanted her.

She moaned into his mouth as he devoured her, reminding himself she was totally real and his. She was not Veronica. She had issues that needed to be taken care of, but he wouldn't send her to the wolves alone next time. He would go with her. Confront her parents. And then they would deal with the outcome together. If they kicked her out of their lives, the loss would be theirs alone. Jason would do everything in his power to help mend the rift for the rest of his life, but he wouldn't compromise his relationship with Libby for anything in the world. Not even her parents.

They were both panting when Jason finally released her lips to draw in oxygen. For a long time, they simply sat there staring at each other with absurd grins, snuggling into each other.

"It would seem there are a number of things I don't know about you," she said. "That makes me feel bad."

He stroked her cheek with one hand and smoothed her

hair back. "My fault. I think I subconsciously didn't talk about myself because I didn't want a repeat with Veronica."

She frowned. "I would never do that. My stupidity and my past are far uglier than yours. It sounds like you had a wholesome childhood in the Midwest."

He rolled his eyes. "Let's not get carried away, but yes, more or less. My parents are hard-working farmers. They would have sent me to college if they could have afforded it. I chose to go into the Army instead. I never asked you about your degree because I didn't want to talk about my lack of one."

"Well, I'm not that shallow, and I don't care about that kind of thing, Jason. I never asked about your education for the same reason. I hate telling people I have a liberal arts degree. It usually causes mocking laughter that hurts deep inside."

He smoothed a hair back from her forehead. "I would never mock you. I'm proud of you. You worked hard and followed your dreams."

"So did you." She lifted an eyebrow.

He smiled. "Yeah, I guess I did."

"I want to hear everything about you. I want to know about your farm and your parents and your childhood. Everything."

"I'll tell you anything you want to know, baby girl, but could we save the twenty questions for after I have my way with you? My cock is hard, and it didn't get what it wanted last night."

She giggled. "We can't have that." Her small hand wiggled between her thigh and his belly until she found his length and stroked him through his jeans. "Let's go inside."

He shook his head. "Can't wait that long." His hands went to her shirt and pulled it over her head. Before she could react, he had her bra unlatched too.

She glanced around, wondering if anyone could see them.

He cupped her chin and brought her face back to center. "My fence is high, and my neighbors don't snoop. Stop worrying about anything but how I'm going to make you scream out your next orgasm in my backyard."

She gasped. "I'm not going to scream anything in your yard, Jason. The whole neighborhood would run over and find me naked if I did so."

He nuzzled her neck, his hands sliding up and down her torso, grazing the undersides of her amazing tits. "We'll see." He flicked his thumbs over her nipples in that way he knew would make her eyes roll back, and then he lifted her off his lap, stood her in front of him, and made quick work of removing the rest of her clothes. Jeans, shoes, thong.

She shivered as she glanced around again.

"Eyes on me, little one. If you can't focus on me and stop worrying about the rest of the world, I'll take you over my knee right here and spank you so hard that your whimpering and pleading will draw the attention of every neighbor."

She pursed her lips adorably.

He released her to rip his T-shirt over his head and then shrug out of his jeans. When he was as naked as her, he turned and settled back on the lounge. "Climb on top of me, baby girl. I want you to ride me while I watch your fucking sexy tits bounce and your mouth fall open when you come."

She obeyed without hesitation, straddling him. She braced herself with her hands on his chest and lined her pussy up with his cock.

"Shit," he muttered. "I don't have a condom."

She shook her head. "I have us covered, Jason. I want to feel you inside me. Just you."

He gripped her hips, keeping her from slamming down on his cock just yet. "Baby, I'll come in two strokes if you do that."

He slid one hand around to cup her bottom. "I've never once had sex without a condom."

She reached for his face and smoothed her fingers over his cheek. "Then it will be a first for both of us."

He held her gaze, not wanting this dream to end if he was still sleeping. "You're mine, Libby."

She nodded. "I'm yours."

"I love you."

"I love you, too."

He slid his hand between them to line his cock up with her pussy and then stroke his fingers through her folds.

He loved the little whimper she made and the way she arched her back and trembled. He took a moment to find her clit and stroke it until it was swollen beneath his fingers. When she started to squirm, he removed his hand and lifted his hips to thrust up into her.

She gasped, her head tipping back.

He'd never seen her look sexier than she did right now. Naked in his backyard. Breasts bouncing as she lifted nearly off him and then slammed back down.

He gritted his teeth against the growing orgasm. He hadn't been kidding. He was going to come in seconds. She felt so damn good on his bare cock.

His groan joined hers, and then he smoothed his hands up to cup her breasts, teasing her sensitive nipples with his fingers.

Libby's mouth fell open wider, and her whimpers filled the air. "Jason…"

"That's it, baby. Take what you need." He slid one hand down to find her clit and stroke it as she pumped faster, bouncing up and down on his lap. The visual alone was enough to make him come. If she were porn, he wouldn't even need to touch himself to reach orgasm. Watching her would be enough.

BECCA JAMESON

Suddenly, she cried out, her body pulsing with her release. He gripped her hips and thrust in deep one last time, letting his orgasm follow right behind hers.

He wasn't sure how much noise either of them made, but his brain cells were completely scrambled when he finally drew in a deep breath and pulled her down to lie against his chest.

He stroked up and down her back, never wanting to pull out of her tight warmth. Never wanting this moment to end. Never wanting to forget how damn perfect she was.

They still had shit to discuss and issues to resolve, but they would handle every one of them together. Because he was never going to let her go, and he certainly would never drive away and leave her standing alone anywhere again.

He closed his eyes, held her tight, and inhaled her scent. "Mine," he whispered.

She whimpered and squirmed against him in response.

He smiled so broadly his cheeks hurt.

CHAPTER 27

Four hours later…

Jason pulled his SUV up to the front of the Garcia home, turned off the engine, and faced Libby, who sat in the passenger seat wringing her hands. He sighed. "We don't have to do this tonight, Libby."

She lifted her gaze to his. "Yes. We do."

A twinge of remorse made him inhale slowly. She was truly distressed. Was he pushing her too hard? He feared she might end up resenting him if he caused a rift between her and her parents. On the other hand, if she couldn't face them and continued to keep him a secret, he would resent her.

She reached out and grabbed his hand, squeezing it. "You don't have to go with me. You could wait in the car." She pursed her lips when she finished speaking, holding her breath.

If he wasn't mistaken, she actually wanted him to go in with her. *Moral support?* "I'm going with you, baby girl. You're not going alone."

She drew in a deep breath and glanced at the house. "Listen, this is likely to go south in a hurry. My mother is going to lose her shit." She lifted her gaze back to Jason and cupped his face. "But that's okay because I realize now that no matter what happens between you and me, I have to stop humoring her. It's not fair to anyone. I would never marry a man my mother set me up with because every time I meet one of her blind dates, I feel defensive and put up a shield no one can penetrate. I have to tell her that her meddling in my life is over. It's my life. I'll choose who I date, and I choose you."

Jason smiled and set his palm over her hand at his face. "I'll be right by your side, little one. I'm proud of you. And I love you. Nothing is going to happen to us. We're solid. We're a team. If your mom can't see her way to accepting the man you've chosen to be with, then your home will be with me."

A tear ran down her face, and she reached to swipe it away. "I love you too." She took a deep breath and let it out.

"You ready?"

"Yep." She released his face and turned to open her door. When she jumped down from his SUV, he was already at her side of the car.

He took her hand and kissed her knuckles.

She smiled at him. It was all going to be all right. No matter what happened here today, she was doing the right thing, and she had an amazing man by her side.

She took a deep breath when they reached the door and then knocked. Usually, she would just walk in, but not this time. Not today. Not with Jason at her side.

It was a Sunday, so she knew her parents would be home. Sure enough, about fifteen seconds later, the door opened. Her father. He smiled and then his brow furrowed. "What are you doing knocking, Libby?"

She shrugged. "Is Mamá here? I need to speak to the two

of you." She wasn't about to beat around the bush here. Time to lay out the cards.

"Of course." He stepped back, holding the door open to let the two of them inside.

Jason lifted a hand. "Jason Nixon, sir. Nice to meet you."

Libby's father looked confused as he politely shook Jason's hand. He'd never been as mistrustful or blatantly racist as her mother. "Ricardo Garcia." He turned toward Libby. "I'll get your mother."

Libby led Jason into the living room and tugged him down to sit next to her on the couch. He glanced down at their combined hands when she didn't release him. She threaded her fingers through his on his thigh and smiled. She was going all-out.

When her parents entered the room a minute later, her mother was smiling, and then her expression fell serious. She literally flinched when she saw Libby's hand in Jason's. "*Qué está pasando, Libertad?*" she asked.

"Don't do that, Mamá. Speak in English," Libby demanded. Her mother had a nasty habit of trying to alienate people by speaking in Spanish in front of them when it suited her.

"Let's sit down," Ricardo said, tugging his wife toward an armchair and then pointing at it. He took the opposite armchair and crossed his legs.

Libby honestly had no idea how her father would react to this bombshell. The man often had little to add to any conversation, which made it difficult to read his true feelings.

"Mamá, this is Jason Nixon. We've been dating for about a month."

Her mother gasped and put a hand over her heart.

Jason squeezed Libby's hand. "Nice to meet you, ma'am."

Maria barely glanced at him before returning her gaze to Libby. "That can't be. You've been dating Eduardo and then Javier."

Libby would bet anything her mother thought by pointing this out she could make Jason flinch. "No, I haven't, Mamá. I started dating Jason the night after I went out with Eduardo. And your stunt last night with Javier was a new low even for you. You came close to breaking us up with your meddling. I won't let that happen again. Jason is my boyfriend. You have to stop setting me up with other men."

Her mother was visibly shaking. "Libertad, you know I don't approve of you dating outside of—"

Libby jerked. "Outside of what, Mamá? Outside of my race? Because even that isn't good enough for you. It's not even a Latino thing for you. My boyfriends have to be specifically from Guatemala with you. Do you not realize how ridiculous that is?"

"People should stick with their own kind," Maria added in her haughty voice.

"Maria," Ricardo interjected. One word. Slightly admonishing, but that was more than nothing. There was hope for her father.

Maria jerked her gaze toward her husband. "What? It worked for you and me, didn't it? I don't see why young people these days think they need to go mixing up with people from other nationalities."

"Mamá. You sound ridiculous. And I didn't come here to argue with you. I came here to tell you that I'm with Jason, so stop sticking your nose in my love life."

Maria crossed her arms and tipped her nose back. "Well, I don't approve."

"Not asking for your approval. I'm *telling* you how things are. From now on, if you want me to come for dinner, you'll invite Jason, too."

Maria gasped. "That's no way to speak to your mother." She started playing with the pearls at her neck.

"Just telling you how it is. Take it or leave it."

"And I think you need to think long and hard about your loyalty to our community, Libertad." She stood. "You can call me when you've come to your senses." She spun around and stomped from the room.

Libby's father rubbed his forehead and then met Libby's gaze. "Give her time, *Mija*."

Libby stood, Jason at her side. "This is how it's going to be, Dad. If you want to see me, Jason is part of the package."

"I understand. I'll talk to your mother, but you know how she is. It won't be easy." He reached out and pulled Libby into his arms. "I love you, *Mija*."

"Thank you, Papá. I love you, too."

When he released her, he held out a hand to Jason again. "Nice to meet you, Jason. Sorry the circumstances are not ideal."

"Nice to meet you too, sir. Hopefully, time will help mend things."

Libby followed Jason out the front door, saying nothing until they were back in the SUV. Finally, she exhaled. "Gotta say, that went better than I expected."

He reached for her hand, a slight smile on his lips. "It did? I'm pretty sure your mom reacted exactly as you suspected."

Libby squeezed his hand. "Yeah, but she could have been worse, and even though my dad didn't say much, he was clearly on my side more than his wife's."

Jason cupped her face and leaned forward to kiss her. "I didn't say much either, baby girl. I didn't want to interfere. I hope that was okay."

"It was perfect. Thank you. You were there for moral support. Now, let's go back to your house. That was stressful. I need to do something to take my mind off my mother."

He wiggled his brows. "I have a few ideas."

She giggled. "Good." She thought she'd feel devastated, but she felt more relief than anything else. There was no doubt in her mind she'd just made the best decision of her life. No more tiptoeing around her mother, lying to make the woman think she was toeing the line. No more blind dates. From now on, Libby was free to be herself whether her mother liked it or not.

CHAPTER 28

Monday morning, Libby was in her kitchen sipping her first cup of coffee when a knock sounded at the door. She groaned, hoping it wasn't another damn gift from Eddie. The man hadn't sent her anything or even texted in over a week and she'd let her guard down.

Libby shuffled slowly toward the door. She should have taken Jason up on his offer to spend the night last night. The only reason she hadn't was because she knew he needed to get to work early today, and she hadn't wanted him to do so on only two hours of sleep. Because the truth was, if she'd stayed, they wouldn't have slept at all.

She was thinking about the way he'd stripped her naked and taken her over his knees when they got back to his house. The feel of his palm on her bottom lingered to this morning, a delicious sensation that had led to one of the best orgasms of her life.

With a smile on her lips, she opened the front door.

Two men stood there. They were huge and dressed in mostly black. Black jeans and T-shirts and boots. They looked fierce and daunting.

"Can I help—"

The one closest to the door flattened his hand on it and pushed it the rest of the way open. Without a word, he stepped inside, his friend behind him.

"Hey, what are you doing?" She jumped back, her coffee sloshing over the edge of the mug to burn her hand. When the men shut the door behind them, she dropped the mug entirely. It shattered, hot coffee splashing her bare legs.

Libby screamed. "Fuck! Get out of here. Who the hell are you?"

The slightly larger of the men grabbed her arm and hauled her toward him, lifting her almost off the floor.

She stopped breathing as she met his menacing glare. Just when she thought he might speak, the second guy grabbed her other arm and held it tight in his grip. She twisted her neck just in time to watch him jab a needle into her biceps.

Full-on panic filled her, and she jerked hard to get away from the men. She screamed as loud as she could, but the first man covered her mouth with his enormous hand.

Her heart raced, and sweat beaded on her forehead. Who the hell were these guys? What did they want from her? She kicked at the man's shins, but her efforts were futile. She was far too small to compete with them, and whatever the man had injected her with was taking effect. She was fading.

She struggled as hard as she could, like a rag doll in the hands of a giant. Fear like nothing she'd ever experienced filled her veins, and then the world went black.

CHAPTER 29

Jason was standing in Tank's office that afternoon when his phone buzzed in his pocket. He pulled it out and answered it without looking. When he was at work, most of the calls that came in were from unknown numbers anyway. Since he was always juggling several clients, he didn't have the luxury of screening calls. "Jason Nixon."

"Jason, it's Christa. Have you talked to Libby today?" Her voice sounded urgent. No, she was freaked out.

Jason instinctively put the phone on speaker. "No. Not since she left my house last night. Is everything okay?"

"No. I don't think so. I got home a few minutes ago, and she's not here. Something's wrong. Jason, I'm freaking out. Something is terribly wrong." Her voice rose every few seconds.

Tank stood and came closer. Sweets and Kraft must have heard them also because they came up behind Jason.

"What makes you think something's wrong, Christa?"

"I knew as soon as I walked in the door. It wasn't locked, and the entryway is covered with coffee. The mug is shattered all over the tile."

Jason's heart stopped. "Did you try calling her?"

"Yes," she wailed. "Her phone is on the kitchen table, and so is her purse. She didn't take her car or anything. Jason, I think someone took her."

"Fuck," Jason muttered. "Get back in your car, okay? I'll be right there."

Tank grabbed his keys. "Let's go." He all but shoved Jason out of his office toward the door. "I'll drive."

Jason could not process what was happening. He was vaguely aware of the fact that he was leaving the office with his coworkers but nothing else.

"I'll take my car, too," Kraft stated. "Sweets is with me. The two of you head to their condo. We'll go to her parents' house." Kraft grabbed Jason's arm. "Address?"

Jason handed his phone to Kraft. "It's the last address in my GPS."

Kraft tapped on the phone several times and handed it back before jogging toward his car.

Jason climbed into the passenger side of Tank's SUV and buckled his seatbelt on autopilot. Thank God the other guys jumped into action. They were all former military after all. Action was their specialty. Jason was numb. Not thinking straight. He needed to pull his head out of his ass and focus.

"Talk to me," Tank said. "Is there anyone who would want to harm Libby?"

Jason ran a hand over his head. The only man he knew who had ever fucked with her was Eddie, but Jesus, would the man kidnap her?

Tank was one step ahead of him. "What about this Eddie guy who's been sending her flowers and shit?"

Jason nodded. "That's where we have to start."

Tank drove as fast as possible without causing them to get pulled over. He jerked the wheel to turn onto the last street hard enough for Jason to grab the door.

Jason was out of the SUV and jogging toward Christa as she got out of her car. She had her arms wrapped around her middle and she was crying.

Tank reached her first and set a hand on her back, so Jason turned and rushed toward the condo. The door was standing open, and Jason pushed it the rest of the way. He stopped breathing as he took in exactly what Christa had described. Coffee everywhere. Shattered ceramic, too. Nothing else was out of the ordinary.

Tank came up behind Jason and looked inside. "No sign of a struggle. I don't think they ever came past the foyer."

Jason ran a hand down his face. "I agree. Fuck." He turned toward Christa. "Call the police. Wait for them. Tell them what you know. Unless you have any other ideas of people who might want to harm her, I suspect Eddie. We're going to head to his house now."

Christa nodded, tears still streaming down her face. "I think she has his address in her phone." She hurried past them and gingerly stepped through the coffee before racing across the room and returning with Libby's phone.

Jason opened it and found Eddie's address under his contact information. He gave it to Tank and then handed the phone back to Christa. "Just in case the cops need it. Or if Libby calls. Jesus. If she calls…"

"I'll call you as fast as I can," Christa assured him. "Go." She was already dialing 911 as Jason and Tank rushed back to the SUV.

Tank drove even faster this time while Jason called Kraft to let him know where they were heading. Kraft was at Libby's parents' house, but neither of her parents had heard from Libby since yesterday when Libby and Jason had visited. Ricardo and Maria were distraught according to Kraft, but Jason didn't have time to deal with them right now.

"Tell them to stay there in case Libby shows up. Christa

called the police. Meet us at the address I'm going to text you."
He ended the call and grabbed the door again as Tank
rounded another corner.

"Glock 9. Glove compartment and another under the seat,"
Tank informed him.

Jason grabbed both and handed one to Tank who shoved it
in the back of his jeans without slowing the car down.

A few minutes later, Tank pulled the car up to a mansion.
Libby had mentioned this place. She hadn't exaggerated. What
Jason didn't understand was if Eddie lived here with his
parents or not. Libby had seemed to think so, but Eddie was a
grown man. No matter how rich daddy was, why would he
still live with his parents?

As they jogged up the front steps, a feeling of dread
crawled up Jason's spine. He didn't like the vibe he got from
this place already.

CHAPTER 30

Libby groaned as she rolled onto her side. Her head was pounding, and she couldn't remember why that might be the case. She hadn't been drinking last night. She'd been with Jason. *Jason…*

She came fully awake, squinting into the room. Her heart rate picked up as she took in her surroundings. *Where the hell am I?* She gasped and tried to sit up as her memory returned. Something was keeping her from moving though. When she tugged on her arms, she realized they were tied together above her head.

Libby twisted her head around to see the rope around her wrists and secured to the headboard. In a full panic, she jerked her gaze around the room. Nothing was familiar. She was in some sort of bedroom, but it had no windows. Just this queen-sized bed, a dresser, and a nightstand. Nothing else.

It was plain and dark. The walls and ceiling were painted black. The furniture was also black. Even the sheets were black. The only reason she could see was because there was a night light plugged into the outlet on the wall across from her. The glow was enough.

She tugged on her hands again, but all she managed to do was scrape her wrists. Already they were sore. She glanced at the rest of her body, wondering if she'd been injured or raped. Relief eased her nerves a tiny fraction when she found herself dressed in the tank top and boxer shorts she'd been wearing when the two giant men had abducted her. Her hair was still in the messy bun she'd slept in, whenever that had been.

She was barefoot, same as when she'd answered the door too, and she wondered how long she'd been here as she recalled the needle and then blackness. They'd fucking drugged her. But why? What was she doing here?

Suddenly the door opened, and someone filled the doorway. At first, all Libby could detect was a silhouette, and she was scared out of her mind. A second later, the man who entered made her nearly swallow her tongue.

"Eddie?"

He smiled as he approached, and then he sat next to her hip and set his hand on her torso.

"What the hell, Eddie? Who were those men, and why am I here?"

He patted her, making her cringe. "Shh. Calm down. You're fine. No one hurt you. No one laid a hand on you while you were sleeping. I promise."

"Untie me. Eddie, fucking untie me right now." She was furious and probably not making the best decisions, but all be damned if she was going to lie here whimpering like a weakling.

His hand lifted from her stomach and then he cupped her face. "Take a breath. I'll untie you as soon as you calm down. You're not a prisoner here. I just wanted some time with you, and you weren't answering my calls."

Like hell I'm not a prisoner here. Does he not know the meaning of the word prisoner? I'm the very fucking definition of prisoner.

She took deep breaths, trying to calm down. Until he

untied her, she wasn't going to be able to do anything at all. She needed to gain his trust in order to figure out how to escape.

"That's my girl."

She flinched. "Don't call me that." Jesus. *I'm not your fucking girl.*

He winced. "Libby... I need you to see that we're a perfect match. That's all."

"And you thought kidnapping me and holding me hostage would help me see reason?" She wished she could control her tongue, but there was no way.

He shook his head. "Don't be so dramatic. Some women fantasize about having a dominant man take them against their will." He chuckled.

Her eyes went wide. Was he fucking serious? And did he really think he was a Dominant? Because she had news for him. He was nothing but a fucking kidnapper. A bully. A piece of shit. He didn't know the meaning of the word Dominant with a capital D.

She tried to calm her racing heart and slow her breathing. "I'm not that kind of woman," she informed him.

He shrugged. "It was worth a try. I was hoping you might enjoy having things a bit rough."

Oh, I do. Just not with you, asshole.

"I've heard a bit of bondage play really spices up a marriage." He wiggled his brows, a ridiculous grin on his lips.

She bit into her lip, forcing herself not to respond.

"Can you be a good girl now so I can untie you?"

She nodded.

He slid his hands up her arms and worked on the knot at her wrists, freeing her a few minutes later.

She gritted her teeth the entire time his hands were on her, pursing her lips, too. She couldn't stand the smell of him, like cheap cologne and fake jewelry. He was wearing three chain necklaces, and they kept swinging against her chin as he worked the knot.

Eddie looked like a gangster. The two times she'd seen him before, he'd been classy but not trashy. Today, he looked more like a drug lord, and she began to wonder if that wasn't the case.

Now that she thought back on the time she went to his house and met his parents, she wondered where all their money came from. Maybe her imagination was getting away with her, but she felt like she was in a mafia film.

The moment Libby's wrists were free she dug her heels into the mattress and shoved herself back against the headboard. She hated that she was wearing nothing more than a tank top and shorts. Her nipples were visible through the thin material.

She pulled her knees up, caring more about covering her breasts than having Eddie see her thighs.

He set his hand on her knee, but she jerked to the left to avoid his touch.

He scowled. "Libertad, you need to listen to reason."

She opened her eyes wide. "No, Eddie, you need to listen to reason. What the fuck is your plan here? Did you think you could have me kidnapped and then just keep me?"

He winced. "Stop saying kidnapped. That's not at all what happened. I sent my men to pick you up because you wouldn't respond to my texts and messages. I need you to listen to reason. If you'd just spend some time with me, you'd see that we are perfect for each other."

"So, your plan is to hold me hostage in this…" she glanced around, trying to decipher where she might be, "…basement? For how long, Eddie? Until I agree to be your girlfriend?" He was certifiable.

He shook his head. "I'm offering far more than that, Libertad. I want you to marry me." He smiled wide.

Oh. Holy. Shit. He was beyond certifiable. "Marry you," she deadpanned.

"Yes. We're a perfect alliance."

She begged to differ.

"You'll see in time that we make sense together. The entire community will attend our wedding. It'll be the biggest event in years."

She stared at him. Did he honestly believe there was a snowball's chance in hell she would ever agree to marry him? If so, and judging by the way he was talking, she needed to keep her mouth shut and figure out a way out of this situation. There was obviously no reasoning with the man.

Eddie's eyes widened. "Hey, I have something for you." He snapped his fingers and rose from the bed.

She watched him walk across the room and through a door she hadn't noticed yet that she assumed might lead to an attached bathroom. She didn't move an inch. Instead, she remained huddled in the corner of the bed against the headboard. She looked around the room again, trying to decide if she could make it to the door before he noticed.

But he was only gone two seconds before he returned holding up a hanger with a black dress on it. "My men retrieved this from your bedroom when they picked you up. I want you to wear it for me. I just know you'll be so very sexy in it."

Libby winced. That "dress" had less material than her current outfit.

He waved her toward him. "Come on. I don't have all day."

She didn't move. Mostly she wasn't sure she could if she wanted to. She was scared out of her mind and fighting to pretend she was anything but. "Eddie, I'm still tired right now. Your men drugged me," she pointed out. "I'm not sure I can even trust my legs to walk across the room yet."

"Don't be ridiculous. You're fine. Get up. You can either go change in the bathroom and maintain your modesty for another few hours until bedtime or I'll help you out of your current clothes and put this on you myself."

She held her breath.

"Or if you'd like, I could have my men come hold you while I cut those clothes off you and leave you naked until dinner time. Which is it?" He started walking toward the door. Were his henchmen in the fucking hallway?

"Fine," she muttered as she slid off the far side of the bed. She shuffled toward him, snatched the silk from his hands, and rushed toward the bathroom before he could try to enter with her. The moment she was clear of the door, she shut it and locked it.

Her heart was racing. God damn it. How was she going to get out of the fucking predicament? If she didn't come up with something fast, she was going to end up in Eddie's bed, and the thought of his skin touching hers made her want to vomit.

She hung the fucking dress on the back of the door and looked in the mirror. Her hair was still in the bun that was now a disaster sticking out all over. She used the toilet and then washed her hands and splashed water on her face.

"Hurry up, Libertad. You have five minutes before I come in there."

Shit. She quickly took off her tank top and shorts before lifting the dress off the hanger and pulling it over her head. *Fuck.* A glance down revealed how low cut the front of the dress was. It showed far too much cleavage and her nipples were insanely obvious.

She was no prude, but this dress was suitable only for a private striptease, and not with the man currently waiting for her on the other side of the door.

He knocked, making her jump. "Time's up."

She took a breath and opened the door, crossing her arms over her chest.

He stepped inside, eyeing her from head to foot and back up. "Panties off. I can see the line of them. It's not attractive. This dress was meant to be worn without undergarments."

She took a step back.

He grabbed her arm and yanked her against his chest. "You're trying my patience, Libertad. Panties off, now, or I tie your wrists to the shower curtain rod and remove them myself. Maybe that's what you want? Is it? Is your pussy already wet for me? I'm beginning to think you're one of those women who enjoy being taken against her will." The corner of his lip lifted in a smirk. "I can play that game if you like it, Libertad. It makes my dick all kinds of hard."

She shook her head. "No. I don't fantasize about rape, Eddie. Let me go." She yanked her arm hard enough to free herself and stepped back until she hit the wall.

He smirked again. "We'll see. Now, take the panties off." He held out a hand.

She'd been scared earlier, but now she was fucking terrified. He was going to end up raping her before this night was over. She could sense it. Her hands were shaking as she reached under the edge of the silk and quickly pulled her thong down her body, hoping she managed it without giving him a glance at her pussy.

His hand was still outstretched, and she reluctantly set the thong in his palm.

He brought it to his nose and inhaled before stuffing them in his pocket.

She held her breath for every second of that, not exhaling until the panties were out of sight. If he had any nose at all, he would have smelled Jason on her panties. She hadn't changed clothes since she left him last night. It had been late when she got home. All she'd done was change into her tank and shorts. The thong would still have remnants of his semen on them.

For some reason it gave her a sense of pleasure knowing that another man's semen was still inside her, still lingered on her pussy. Fuck Eddie.

"Now take your hair down and fix it. I like it loose, down your back." He pointed at the vanity. "Everything you'll need is in the drawers." He leaned against the doorframe. "Hurry. I don't have all day."

She shoved off the wall and started going through the drawers until she found a brush. Her hands were shaking as she took the thick band out of her hair and then started working the brush through the knotted mess.

Think, Libby. You have to get yourself out of this house. No one knows where you are. She groaned inside her head as she pictured her phone on the kitchen table, the phone that Jason could have used to track her.

Is he looking for me yet? She didn't know what time it was or how long she'd been out from being drugged, but she did know Christa had been due home in the early afternoon. And Libby nearly smiled when she remembered the coffee and the shattered mug. Christa would know something was wrong the moment she got home. How long ago was that?

Eddie spoke of having dinner later, so she had to assume she'd only been asleep a few hours. Maybe she could convince him to let her out of this room. If he locked her inside, she didn't stand much of a chance. It was doubtful anyone would hear her screaming from wherever this basement was.

CHAPTER 31

Jason's phone buzzed in his pocket as he reached the front door of the Lopez mansion. He yanked it out and read a text from Christa.

> *We were wrong. Whoever took Libby did go farther into the condo. They ransacked her room and took the dress Eddie sent her.*

"Fuck," Jason muttered. He glanced at Tank. "Eddie has her."

Tank nodded, not asking for more information as Jason pounded on the front door.

He had to wonder if Eddie really lived here with his parents. It seemed incredibly unlikely that he'd kidnapped Libby and brought her to his parents' home, but this was where they needed to start.

He knocked again, several times, not waiting long in between before he did it again. By the time a thin, older man opened the door, Tank was next to Jason.

The man looked annoyed. "Can I help you?"

"Is this where Eddie Lopez lives?"

"May I ask who's inquiring?"

"No, you may not fucking ask—"

Tank set a hand on Jason's biceps. "We're looking for Eddie the son, not the father. Does he live here?"

"None of your business." The man started to close the door.

Tank stuck out his foot and stopped him, slamming his hand on the door at the same time. "I'm sorry, sir, but this is important. A woman is missing, and we think she's with Eddie."

The man gasped and took a step back. "There's no woman here."

"Her name is Libertad Garcia. You met her the other day," Jason pointed out, grateful that Libby had given him all the details about her encounter with the Lopez family.

The man nodded. "I know Libertad. Eddie's girlfriend. If she's with him, she wouldn't be missing. But I haven't seen her today."

Another man came from deeper in the house. "What's going on, Franco?"

"These men are looking for Eddie's girlfriend. They're incredibly rude, too. Shoved their way into the house."

The man's expression went from curiosity to fury in seconds. He rushed the rest of the way forward and tried to shove Tank out of the way. Fat chance of that happening. There was a reason the man's nickname was Tank.

Jason planted his hand on the door and gave it a firm shove at the same time, ensuring they could not be shut out of the house. "Look, the police are on their way here. They'll be here any moment. You can either help us or wait for them. Your choice, but time is of the essence here. Is Eddie home?"

The man came closer, puffing out his chest. "Get the fuck out of my house right now."

Jason stepped inside, shoving the man out of the way. He

started storming deeper into the house, glancing in every direction. He didn't give a single fuck that he was breaking the law. Instinct told him Libby was here.

"What the fuck do you think you're doing?" Eduardo said.

Jason didn't respond.

"My son doesn't live in the main house, you fucking asshole. I haven't seen him today. He's surely at work. Most people work during the day."

Jason turned around. "Where does he work?"

"None of your business."

Jason stared at the older Eduardo for a second. Something else the man said had caught his attention. "Main house? Is there another house on the property?"

"Fuck you," Eduardo shouted.

Tank grabbed the man by the shirt and slammed him against the wall. "Where the fuck is your son? Start talking."

A woman screamed.

Jason spun around to find her rushing forward. A classy-looking woman dressed in extremely expensive clothing like Eduardo. Jason thought she must Eddie's mother.

She screamed again. "Eduardo, what are these men doing here?"

"Go back to the kitchen, Elena," Eduardo told her.

Jason approached her. "Tell me where your son is, ma'am."

"Eddie? I assume he's at work." She put her hand over her heart. "What do you want with my son?"

"I believe he kidnapped my girlfriend this morning."

She gasped. "You must be mistaken. Why would he do that? He has his own girlfriend."

Jason shook his head. "No, he does not. He has mine."

Two large men came running from deeper in the house, both wearing all black. What the fuck kind of people were these?

The men were big though, almost as big as Tank and Jason.

Jason pulled his gun out of the back of his jeans and held it up, praying to God they weren't wrong about this. Jesus. Fuck. They were in deep now. But his gut told him things were not on the up and up here.

Fucking mansion with a fucking butler and two bodyguards? Mafia. Drug cartel. Something illegal. Money was dripping off the walls in this place.

One of the men reached for his back.

"Don't you fucking move an inch. Stay right there," Jason shouted.

The man held up his hands. So did his partner.

"Where the fuck is she?" Jason shouted.

The men glanced at each other, pissing Jason the fuck off.

Tank was still holding the elder Eduardo by the shirt as he dragged the man past Jason and deeper into the house. Elena stood whimpering in the corner of the hallway, clutching the front of her blouse.

"Hatch," Tank shouted. "There's a fucking guest house in back."

One of the two men suddenly bent forward and rammed his full body into Jason, knocking the breath out of him. Jason barely kept his grip on his gun.

Jason righted himself and came after the bastard, swinging a hard left hook that knocked the guy against the wall. He slammed his head hard enough into the drywall that it cracked as the guy slid to the ground.

The second man charged next, pulling his gun.

Jason swung around and kicked the gun out of his grip, sending it flying before Jason landed a punch to the guy's stomach. While he was doubled over, Jason grabbed his shirt and kneed him hard in the face. These assholes didn't know who the fuck they were messing with.

Elena was screaming again, but Jason gave her a hard look.

"Shut the fuck up. Where is your son? Does he live in the guest house?"

She nodded. "Yes, but if he's done something, I don't know anything about it."

Sure she didn't. Jason didn't give a single fuck right now. All he cared about was rescuing Libby from Eddie. He made sure the two men were out cold and then jogged deeper into the house.

Tank still had a grip on Eduardo, who was putting up a fight near the back door. "Listen, old man, I don't want to have to hurt you, but I fucking will if you don't knock it off."

The guy kept struggling.

Jason glanced around and then reached for a long, elegant cord that was holding back the expensive drapes. It was meant to be decorative, but today it was about to be useful. He grabbed a chair from the kitchen table and shoved it against Eduardo's knees, forcing the man to sit.

"*Stop*," Elena screamed. "Don't hurt him. He doesn't know anything."

Jason ignored her as he tossed the rope to Tank.

Footsteps rushing into the room made Jason spin around to find Sweets and Kraft joining them.

"About time you got here," Tank joked. "Go, Hatch. We've got this. Sweets and Kraft can secure the goons in the hallway. Go find Libby." He nodded toward the back door as he jerked Eduardo's hands behind his back.

Jason yanked open the door and left it open as he jogged out the back. He spotted a second house beyond the pool. He rounded the pool and ran toward the house.

He didn't bother knocking this time. He kicked the front door in on the first try. It splintered and swung hard against the wall.

Someone screamed. The sweetest voice he'd ever heard.

He ran toward the noise, trying to pinpoint where it was coming from.

"Downstairs," she yelled, the second half of the word muffled. If that fucker hurt her...

Jason found the door to the basement on the other side of the kitchen. It was standing open. He took the stairs two at a time, gun drawn. When he hit the bottom, he found Eddie at the foot of the stairs. The guy was holding Libby's back against his front. He had a hand against her neck, and he was swinging a knife around.

"Get the fuck out of my house," Eddie shouted.

Libby's eyes were wide, and she was struggling, but she looked unharmed. If this asshole hurt one hair on her body...

"Drop the knife, Eddie," Jason said, keeping his voice calm. He could easily take this man out. He was trained to kill in situations like this. Eddie was making it far too easy. He wasn't even holding the knife at Libby's throat, and he didn't appear to have a gun.

Hell, even if he had a gun to her temple, Jason could kill him with one shot to the head and end this game, but that kind of action would traumatize Libby for the rest of her life. He didn't want to kill Eddie if he could avoid it.

"Fuck you," Eddie sputtered, his spittle flying through the air. "She's mine."

Jason kept inching closer. He glanced at Libby again to make sure she wasn't in shock. She was close, but not there yet.

"Put the knife down, Eddie. This is over. The police are on their way. If you end this peacefully, it will be much easier on you. If you hurt her, you'll end up with the death penalty."

Eddie was shaking. That was a good sign. He was fucking crazy. He tightened his grip on Libby's neck, pulling her almost off the ground.

She grabbed his forearms, trying to free herself.

Fuck. Jason didn't want to have to shoot Eddie. "You can't get out of this, man. I was on a special forces team with the Army. So were my friends in the main house. You don't stand a chance. Put. The. Knife. Down."

Eddie's fingers tightened again as Jason shifted his focus to the man's other hand. He followed the pattern as Eddie swung the knife back and forth. He needed to put an end to this, and he wanted to do it without killing Eddie.

The moment his arm was on the backswing, Jason was ready. His plan was risky. If he misjudged by even a few inches, Libby could be severely injured.

And...*now.* Jason swung his foot around and kicked the knife out of Eddie's hand. It went flying across the room, and Jason lunged forward, slamming his fist into the side of Eddie's head while his attention was on his injured wrist.

The second he made contact, Eddie's grip released.

Libby slid downward, but Jason caught her and pulled her away from Eddie as her assailant crumpled to the floor. Thank God. Jason didn't want to have to continue pummeling the asshole.

Libby was gasping for air as Jason hugged her against his chest. He finally released her just enough to hold her face and look into her eyes. "Are you hurt, baby?"

She rubbed her neck but shook her head. "No. I'm fine."

Relieved, he pulled her against his chest again.

"You found me," she whispered, her body shaking violently.

"Yeah." He was choked up himself. Emotions flooded him now that the adrenaline rush was passing. He'd rescued dozens of people in his military career, but none that mattered to him as much as Libby. None he was in love with.

Several voices came from upstairs.

"Down here," Jason shouted. "It's over."

Feet pounded on the stairs. Police. Four of them. They had

their guns drawn, but they holstered them as soon as they realized Jason had already knocked out the assailant.

Jason hated thinking about all the damn questions and red tape they were about to endure. Hours of questioning and statements, but at least Libby was safe. She was in his arms. He was never going to let her go. He would be by her side the entire day.

There was just one problem. He found Tank coming down the stairs behind the police. "Could you find something Libby could put on?"

His woman was shivering against him, and he knew she would still be shivering even after he wrapped her in more clothing. She was in shock more than anything, but there wasn't a chance in hell he was going to have her spend the day in this ridiculous dress that barely passed for lingerie while everyone stared at her.

"On it." Tank nodded and headed down the hallway.

CHAPTER 32

Libby was still shaking four hours later when they finally got back to Jason's house. She was drained, and couldn't muster up the energy to open the passenger door.

It didn't matter. Jason was there in seconds. He reached into the car and unbuckled her before grinning. "Mind if just this once I lift you out of the car?"

She smiled back, grateful he could find some humor in a very shitty day. "I'd like that, but don't make a habit of it."

He stuck one hand under her knees and the other behind her back and lifted her into his arms.

She leaned into him, wrapping her arms around his neck as he carried her inside.

Without stopping, he continued straight through to the master bathroom and sat on the edge of the tub. He reached in and turned on the water.

She sighed. "Good idea. I'm so fucking tired, but I want to wash this day off first."

He stood her next to him and eased the thick sweater off her shoulders. It had provided her with cover and warmth all evening. Beneath it was the stupid black dress.

"May I?" Jason asked as he reached for the hem.

His hesitation both endeared him to her and also pissed her off. She cupped his cheeks. "I'm fine."

He held her gaze. "I know you think you are, and I know you told the police that Eddie didn't touch you, but I also know it doesn't take much for a woman to be traumatized for a long time after what you've been through. I won't contribute to your terror."

She leaned closer and kissed him gently. "I'm fine, Jason. I need you to touch me. Erase this day with your touch. Dominate me in that way you do that tells me I'm yours and I'm safe and I'm loved."

He smiled and then cupped her face and kissed her so hard she nearly fell over backward. When he was done, he met her gaze again. "God, I love you."

"I love you, too."

He pulled the dress over her head and dropped it on the floor. His gaze roamed her body, inspecting her for injuries. She knew this, and she let him, saying nothing. Except for minor rope burns on her wrists and bruising at her neck, she was fine.

When he was satisfied, she grabbed the hem of his shirt and pulled it over his head. "Join me."

"You sure?"

"Positive." She reached for the button on his jeans next, but her hands were shaking. He eased them away and finished undressing himself.

His glorious cock caught her attention and sent arousal through her body. She bit her lip as he stepped into the tub and then lifted her by the waist over the edge. He settled against the end of the tub and spread his legs, reaching for her.

She let out a long, slow breath as she relaxed between his legs, her back against his chest, her breasts above his forearm. She leaned her head back on his shoulder. She needed to talk about the day for a while, and she hoped he wouldn't mind.

"Jason..."

"What, baby girl? Go ahead." He stroked her arm, letting her know he was taking things at her speed tonight.

"I can't believe Eddie had his goons kidnap me," she began. "I can't believe Eddie *had* goons."

"I didn't see that coming either, little one."

"I can't believe you knocked them all out with your bare hands." She twisted to grin at him. "Holy shit. You're fucking Rambo."

He chuckled. "Hardly, but it's what I was trained to do." He shrugged.

"Do you really think his parents knew nothing about his plan?"

Jason shrugged. "I'm not sure. The police will have to sort it out. They have much bigger problems than that on their hands. The Lopez family has been on the FBI's radar for months. It seems they have ties to a cartel. I'm betting Eddie was being groomed to become the next Lopez drug king. Apparently, Eddie was used to getting everything he wanted. And when you turned him down, he wasn't willing to accept no for an answer."

"I can't believe I didn't realize what a dick he was the first night we went out. I mean, I knew I didn't care for him or his friends, but I didn't pin him for a drug lord. Nor did I expect him to have me kidnapped." She sighed and relaxed closer to Jason's huge, warm body. He made her feel safe and secure. She was going to need that for a few days.

Christa had called their boss at Open Skies and let them know what had happened even before her shift was supposed to start today. She would take the rest of this week off and then reevaluate.

"I'm not going to let you out of my sight for days. I hope you can live with that," Jason murmured against her forehead.

"Counting on it." She chuckled as she remembered something else that had happened today and twisted to face him again. "Oh my God, my *mom.*"

He grinned.

"She fucking hugged you."

He chuckled. "She did. Though I must say, I would rather have spent two years winning her over than have you go through what you went through today."

"I know, but holy shit. She is going to spend a decade apologizing for being so hard on you and for setting me up with Eddie in the first place, and then begging me to continue seeing him." She twisted farther and set her hand on Jason's cheek. "You won her over."

He laughed again, his body shaking so much that the water sloshed around them. "Yeah, mothers always fall right into my palm when I rescue their daughters from the arms of a madman."

She swatted playfully at his chest and then scrambled to turn all the way around and straddle him.

He set his hands on her hips as she lowered her butt to his thighs. "Baby girl…" he warned.

"I need you." If he fucking turned her down, she would be devastated.

He slid his hands up her body and cupped her breasts. "You're sure?"

She moaned as his thumbs stroked her nipples, and then she tipped her head back. "Positive. Make it all go away. Replace it."

He pinched her nipples, and she thrust her pussy forward to stroke against his cock.

"Uh-uh." He slid her body away from his erection, putting a few inches of space between them.

She lowered her gaze to his. "Jason..." she whimpered.

"Don't worry, little one. I'm going to fuck you so hard you won't remember any man ever touching you before me, but I'll do it on my terms. Understood?"

She shuddered. "Yes, Sir." Her nipples hardened further, and she gripped his legs with her inner thighs.

"Good girl." He cupped her breasts again, weighing them.

She sighed, resigning herself to the fact that he wasn't in a hurry. A fast fuck was not what she was going to get tonight.

His hands slid down her body and landed on her thighs, his thumbs stroking the sensitive skin close to her pussy. "Are you wet for me, baby girl?"

"Yes, Sir."

He stroked through her folds, making her gasp. He was moving too slow. Achingly slow. Touching her reverently as if they'd never had sex before. He explored her labia and her clit, not touching her hard enough or long enough in any one spot.

Finally, when she thought she might have to resort to begging, he thrust two fingers into her while reaching for his cock with his other hand. He stroked up and down. "Is this what you want, Libby?"

"Yes, Sir. Please."

"Tell me."

"Please let me fuck your cock. Right here in the tub. Let me ride you. I need you inside me so badly." She watched as he stroked the tip with his thumb. It was so hot when he touched himself like that. He was so confident and controlling at all times.

Finally, he released his grip and lifted her by the hips. "Okay, little one. Ride me. Hands on my shoulders. I want to watch your tits bounce as you grind your pussy against my cock."

Her mouth fell open as he let her body slowly lower over his erection until she was filled with him. It wasn't until she was sitting against his thighs that he released her and grabbed the edges of the tub. "Ride me, Libby."

She eagerly obeyed his demand, grabbing his shoulders and lifting herself almost off his cock before impaling herself again. *God, this feels good.* He rarely let her control things like this, and it nearly brought tears to her eyes when she considered why he was doing this.

He'd manipulated her into being completely under his command while giving her the reins. He was fully dominating her, but not in a way that might scare her tonight. And she loved him for it. It empowered her to fuck him harder. Faster. She lifted and lowered with so much force that water sloshed all around them.

Her arousal grew by the second, drowning out the shitshow of a day. It felt so fucking good. And when her pussy clenched around his cock, gripping him with her release, she cried out and kept pumping.

She didn't stop until Jason grabbed her hips to steady her. She dropped her gaze to his and watched his own release reveal itself in his expression. Mouth open. Eyes unseeing. Breath hitching. And finally, that low moan he emitted every time he came.

She did that to him.

He did this to her.

When she couldn't hold her body up any longer, she slumped against his chest as his hands roamed up and down her back. "Thank you, Sir," she whispered.

"You're welcome, little one."

The water was growing cold, but she didn't have the energy to move. Instead, she hugged him, wrapping her arms around his neck and holding him close. "Please burn that dress."

"First thing in the morning." He chuckled.

For a long time, she continued to lie there, relaxing slowly, the tension easing from her body as his hands roamed over her. It was comforting. She knew he was waiting for her to decide when she wanted to get out, and she fought the tears of joy and love that welled up inside her. "I love you," she murmured.

"I love you too, baby girl."

"I might say that a lot this week."

"I might too," he responded. "We don't have to keep a tally."

She sighed heavily. "I just need a few more minutes before we get out."

"Take all the time you want. I can hold you like this all night." His leg shifted, and a moment later, the water came back on. He was adding hot water to the tub.

She was the luckiest woman on earth.

EPILOGUE

One month later…

Jason was yanked out of sleep when the bed shifted and Libby's gasp filled the room. He immediately turned toward her, finding her sitting upright, her chest rising and falling.

He set his hand on her back to help ground her. This was a frequent occurrence. The nightmares. For the first few weeks after her kidnapping, she'd woken up screaming at least once a night. In the last few weeks, her nightmares had become less frequent.

"I'm right here, Libby," he soothed, letting his hand slide up her back. "You're okay."

She turned toward him, drawing in a long deep breath before lowering onto the bed, facing him. "Sorry." She set a hand on his cheek.

"Don't be sorry, baby girl. I've got you." He pulled her closer so that their bodies were aligned and brushed the hair from her forehead. He could see her perfectly well since he'd put a nightlight in the room weeks ago.

She rarely slept at her condo anymore. In fact, the lease was almost up, and she would be moving in with him permanently soon. "That one was different. You didn't scream. Want to talk about it?"

Her brow was furrowed for a moment and then she surprised him with a slow smile. "It wasn't the abduction. It was my mother this time."

He groaned. "Your mother? You stress out about her enough when you're awake. Now she's infiltrating your dreams?" They'd come a long way in the past month. Maria Garcia had even been civil toward Jason. She'd even looked him in the eye a few times without scowling. He knew she still wasn't pleased with his existence, but she kept her mouth shut. Her gratitude for his part in rescuing Libby outweighed her ingrained dislike for his skin color and country of origin.

Libby sighed and wiggled even closer to Jason. "We were at the dinner table, and she pretended to accidentally spill most of the pot of coffee on your lap."

He chuckled. They were going to Libby's parents' house for dinner tomorrow night. It wasn't surprising that Libby was anxious about it. Her mother would undoubtedly say something that would get under Libby's skin. "I'll be sure to put my napkin in my lap to protect my skin just in case," he joked.

She groaned. "I hate that she gets under my skin."

Jason rubbed her back. "Baby girl, she's your mom. They are supposed to get under your skin. She's come a long way. Last time we went over there, she didn't growl at me a single time. She even offered me a glass of water."

Libby drew in a breath, holding my gaze. "I love you. Thanks for putting up with me."

Jason flattened his palm between her shoulder blades and kissed her lips. "I love you too, and I'd put up with anything as long as I have you in my life. Are we going to tell her you're moving in?"

Libby smiled and wiggled her eye brows. "Already did."

Jason gasped, his eyes going wide. "You did? You told her? When?"

"The other day when I went by to get my photo albums. Slipped it right into the conversation like it was no big deal. You'd think I was an adult and all," she teased.

He was stunned and pleased. "How'd she take it?"

Libby shrugged. "She didn't say a word for a while and then changed the subject. I think she decided to pretend I never spoke. It's possible she won't acknowledge it at any point, but the important thing is that I told her. I left your address on the kitchen table too. At least she has it and knows where to find me."

"I'm proud of you." Jason pressed his lips to hers again, this time deepening the kiss as he rolled her to her back and threaded their fingers together. She had no idea how happy it made him that she'd taken the initiative and told her mom about her upcoming move.

He loved Libby to pieces, and every gesture she made like that reminded him that she loved him too. All he asked for was for her to put him first, and she did. Every day.

They were also planning a trip to visit his parents in Iowa soon. His mother was thrilled to learn that he had a serious girlfriend. Jason couldn't wait to bring her home and share that side of him with the woman he loved.

When he finally broke from her lips, she was panting. He stared at her face, smiling. She blinked at him. "What?"

He stroked her knuckles with his thumb. "I was just thinking about how lucky I am."

She returned the smile. "I feel damn lucky myself. Now, are you going to finish what you started? Or were you planning to leave me all hot and bothered and go back to sleep?"

He chuckled as he pressed his erection against her thigh. "Believe me, I have every intention of ravaging your body, even if it is the middle of the night. Who needs sleep anyway?"

He didn't let her respond. Instead, he resumed kissing her, this time coming up over her body while pressing her hand into the pillow above her head. He'd give up sleep any night of the week if it meant that he got to remind Libby how much he loved her with his lips, his tongue, his hands, and his cock.

It was working. She was moving in with him. God, he loved this woman.

AUTHOR'S NOTE

I hope you've enjoyed *Layover* from my Open Skies series. Please enjoy the following excerpt from *Redeye*, the second book in the series.

REDEYE

OPEN SKIES, BOOK TWO

"Are you sure this is a good idea?" Christa asked as she stood in her bedroom, staring at herself in the full-length mirror on the back of her door. "I don't even know this guy."

Libby laughed from where she sat on Christa's bed, leaning against the headboard. "You asked Jason to set you up with someone on more than one occasion. Now that it's tonight, you have cold feet?"

Christa sighed, wondering if the dress she'd chosen was too much for a first date. They were just going to dinner. Would he think she was working too hard to impress him if she wore this black dress? Maybe she should change into jeans.

"You're overthinking it," Libby said. "I can see your mind working from here."

Christa spun around. "You know how I am. I'm an introvert. Yes, in theory, I want to go out with this buff, sexy, military friend of Jason's, but in practice I'm nervous. Plus, we're in the middle of packing, and I have to work three shifts still this week, all of them are redeyes, and I'm a horrible conversationalist."

Libby spun around and sat on the edge of the bed. "You'll be fine. Jason says Kraft is an extrovert. He can carry the conversation. Besides, you've technically already met him. You danced with him at Destiny's wedding."

Christa groaned. "That doesn't count. I can't even remember it well. Just some large guy who swung me around the floor. We didn't exchange many words."

Libby glanced around. "Well, don't worry about the packing. It's mostly done. We don't move out until Saturday. You'll have the days to stuff the last few things into boxes. And then you can nap and get to the airport."

Libby made it sound simple. Christa felt a bit overwhelmed. Why had she agreed to a blind date on a Monday night with so much going on? In addition, she felt bad about leaving Libby home alone to pack. Between Christa, Bex, and Shayla, they usually made sure their schedules included never leaving Libby alone. If Jason couldn't be with her, one of them always was.

Ever since a crazy man she'd gone on one date with abducted Libby and held her in his basement, they all worried she might freak out if she stayed in the townhouse by herself for any length of time.

Christa felt guilty leaving her. "You sure you're okay with me going out? I could cancel. There's no reason I need to go on a blind date tonight of all nights."

Libby waved a hand through the air. "Don't be silly. I'm fine. I'm just going to watch old reruns and finish packing the kitchen."

The doorbell rang.

Christa took a deep breath. "You're sure?" she asked again.

"Positive. Get your shoes." She pointed at Christa's feet.

Christa headed across the room to grab her heels. Half the reason she'd chosen a dress was so that she could wear heels. She was five-foot-six, but she remembered Kraft was six-foot.

"I'll let him in." Libby slid off the bed and rushed from the room, bounding down the stairs two at a time, the way she often took the stairs.

Christa took a deep breath and wandered back into the bathroom. She stared at herself in the mirror again. Her pale blond hair was almost white. She was wearing it down tonight because she knew it was one of her best features. It was wavy and long and always attracted attention. She wondered how long it would take Kraft to ask her if it was natural.

She applied another coat of lip gloss and pinched her cheeks. Her pale skin lacked color, but that wouldn't last long because soon she would be embarrassed for any number of reasons and then her cheeks would flush a deep shade of red. There was nothing she could do to stop it.

Finally, she spun and headed for the stairs, praying this blind date wasn't about to be the worst decision of her life.

ALSO BY BECCA JAMESON

Open Skies:

Layover

Redeye

Nonstop

Standby

Delta Team Three (Special Forces: Operation Alpha):

Destiny's Delta

Canyon Springs:

Caleb's Mate

Hunter's Mate

Corked and Tapped:

Volume One: Friday Night

Volume Two: Company Party

Volume Three: The Holidays

Surrender:

Raising Lucy

Teaching Abby

Leaving Roman

Choosing Kellen

Pleasing Josie

Honoring Hudson

Nurturing Britney

Project DEEP:

Reviving Emily

Reviving Trish

Reviving Dade

Reviving Zeke

Reviving Graham

Reviving Bianca

Reviving Olivia

Project DEEP Box Set One

Project DEEP Box Set Two

SEALs in Paradise:

Hot SEAL, Red Wine

Hot SEAL, Australian Nights

Hot SEAL, Cold Feet

Dark Falls:

Dark Nightmares

Club Zodiac:

Training Sasha

Obeying Rowen

Collaring Brooke

Mastering Rayne

Trusting Aaron

Claiming London

Sharing Charlotte

Taming Rex

Tempting Elizabeth

Club Zodiac Box Set One

Club Zodiac Box Set Two

The Art of Kink:

Pose

Paint

Sculpt

Arcadian Bears:

Grizzly Mountain

Grizzly Beginning

Grizzly Secret

Grizzly Promise

Grizzly Survival

Grizzly Perfection

Arcadian Bears Box Set One

Arcadian Bears Box Set Two

Sleeper SEALs:

Saving Zola

Spring Training:

Catching Zia

Catching Lily

Catching Ava

Spring Training Box Set

The Underground series:

Force

Clinch

Guard

Submit

Thrust

Torque

The Underground Box Set One

The Underground Box Set Two

Saving Sofia (Special Forces: Operations Alpha)

Wolf Masters series:

Kara's Wolves

Lindsey's Wolves

Jessica's Wolves

Alyssa's Wolves

Tessa's Wolf

Rebecca's Wolves

Melinda's Wolves

Laurie's Wolves

Amanda's Wolves

Sharon's Wolves

Wolf Masters Box Set One

Wolf Masters Box Set Two

Claiming Her series:

The Rules

The Game

The Prize

Emergence series:

Bound to be Taken

Bound to be Tamed

Bound to be Tested

Bound to be Tempted

Emergence Box Set

The Fight Club series:

Come

Perv

Need

Hers

Want

Lust

The Fight Club Box Set One

The Fight Club Box Set Two

Wolf Gatherings series:

Tarnished

Dominated

Completed

Redeemed

Abandoned

Betrayed

Wolf Gatherings Box Set One

Wolf Gathering Box Set Two

Durham Wolves series:

Rescue in the Smokies

Fire in the Smokies

Freedom in the Smokies

Stand Alone Books:

Blind with Love

Guarding the Truth

Out of the Smoke

Abducting His Mate

Three's a Cruise

Wolf Trinity

Frostbitten

A Princess for Cale/A Princess for Cain

ABOUT THE AUTHOR

Becca Jameson is a USA Today best-selling author of over 100 books. She is well-known for her Wolf Masters series, her Fight Club series, and her Club Zodiac series. She currently lives in Houston, Texas, with her husband and her Goldendoodle. Two grown kids pop in every once in a while too! She is loving this journey and has dabbled in a variety of genres, including paranormal, sports romance, military, and BDSM.

A total night owl, Becca writes late at night, sequestering herself in her office with a glass of red wine and a bar of dark chocolate, her fingers flying across the keyboard as her characters weave their own stories.

During the day--which never starts before ten in the morning!--she can be found jogging, running errands, or reading in her favorite hammock chair!

...*where Alphas dominate*...

Becca's Newsletter Sign-up

Join my Facebook fan group, Becca's Bibliomaniacs, for the most up-to-date information, random excerpts while I work, giveaways, and fun release parties!

Facebook Fan Group:
Becca's Bibliomaniacs

Contact Becca:
www.beccajameson.com
beccajameson4@aol.com

facebook.com/becca.jameson.18
twitter.com/beccajameson
instagram.com/becca.jameson
bookbub.com/authors/becca-jameson
goodreads.com/beccajameson
amazon.com/author/beccajameson

Printed in Great Britain
by Amazon

66777380R00139